MARVEL

AVENGERS

Storybook Collection

MARVEL

Los Angeles
New York

CONTENTS

MarvelHQ.com

© 2018 MARVEL

"Avengers Assemble! Part One" adapted by Colin Hosten from "Here to Infinity" written by Andy Schmidt. Illustrated by Carlo Barberi.

"Avengers Assemble! Part Two" adapted by Colin Hosten from "Here to Infinity" written by Andy Schmidt. Illustrated by Carlo Barberi.

"The Doom of Fin Fang Foom!" written by Alexandra West. Illustrated by Roberto DiSalvo.

"Blue Steel" adapted by Alexandra West from "Iron Man Beginnings" written by Jim McCann. Illustrated by Khoi Pham.

"She-Hulk SMASH!" written by Andy Schmidt. Illustrated by Carlo Barberi.

"Training Day" adapted by Alexandra West from "Captain America Beginnings" written by Jim McCann. Illustrated by Michael Ryan.

"A Heroic Little Helper" written by Colin Hosten. Illustrated by Aurelio Mazzara and Gaetano Petrigno.

"Pint-Size Power" written by Ivan Cohen. Illustrated by Ario Anindito.

"Time Warp Teamwork" written by Alexandra West. Illustrated by Dario Brizuela and Gaetano Petrigno.

"The Legend of Black Panther" adapted by Alexandra West from "The Legend of Black Panther" written by Andy Schmidt. Illustrated by Simone Buonfantino.

"Mixed Signals from Knowhere" written by Colin Hosten. Illustrated by Aurelio Mazzara and Stefano Landini.

"Ultron Goes Viral" written by Calliope Glass. Illustrated by Cucca Vincenzo and Salvatore Di Marco.

"The Incredible Spider-Hulk" written by Arie Kaplan. Illustrated by Simone Buonfantino.

"The New Squirrel in Town" written by Calliope Glass. Illustrated by Aurelio Mazzara and Gaetano Petrigno.

"Klaw's Revenge" written by Andy Schmidt. Illustrated by Simone Buonfantino.

"From Here to Infinity" adapted by Alexandra West from "From Here to Infinity" written by Andy Schmidt. Illustrated by Carlo Barberi.

"A Marvelous Duo" adapted by Alexandra West from "Ms. Marvel's Fists of Fury" written by Calliope Glass. Illustrated by Caravan Studios.

"Island of the Cyborgs" written by Ray Caban. Illustrated by Eduardo Mello.

For information address Marvel Press, 125 West End Avenue, New York, New York, 10023.

First Edition, April 2018

11 10 9 8 7 6 5 4 3 2

FAC-038091-18298

Printed in the United States of America

Stories painted by Tommaso Moscardin, Fabio Pacuilli, Pierluigi Cosolano, Matt Milla, Ekaterina Myshalova, Nataliya Torretta, Vita Efremova, Anna Beliashova, Matteo Baldrighi, Olga Lepaieva, Ekaterina Myshalova, Stefani Rennee, Alesia Barsukova, and Davide Mastrolonardo.

Cover illustrated by Eduardo Mello
Cover painted by Davide Mastrolonardo

Storybook designed by David Roe

Library of Congress Control Number: 2017955293

ISBN: 978-1-4847-2957-1

Visit www.MarvelHQ.com

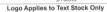

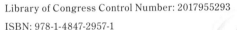

Avengers Assemble!
Part One

HIDDEN WITHIN AN ORDINARY WORLD

are those who are extraordinary. They are called Super Heroes. They rise up to defeat evil and keep the world safe. Tony Stark is one of those heroes.

A genius and a billionaire, Tony created a suit made of iron. People came to know him as Iron Man. "I took care of them for ya, Rogers!" Iron Man radioed, as he destroyed a fleet of escaping villains. "No need to thank me."

"Well, let me return the favor," Steve Rogers replied as he swiftly took out two guards on the ground.

When the Army recruited Steve Rogers, they infused him with a serum that made him a Super Soldier. Steve was also given a shield made of Vibranium, the strongest metal in the world. With it, he became known as the Super Hero Captain America.

Back at their base of operations, two more Super Heroes were busy combat training.

"In Russia, I was taught to never be caught unprepared," Natasha Romanoff said, practicing her roundhouse kick. "And I will teach you the same, Clint."

"Tasha! I'm not a little kid. I don't need to be taught," Clint Barton replied. "If you remember, I grew up learning all of my necessary skills at the circus."

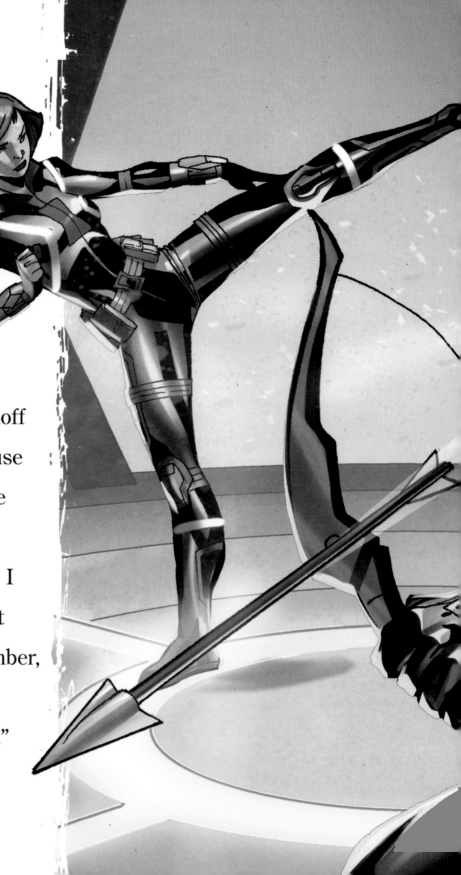

Clint shot three consecutive arrows at a target across the room, hitting the bullseye each time. He turned to Natasha. "Plus, hand-to-hand combat isn't really my style. I much prefer archery to kicking."

Clint Barton was an expert marksman. Eventually he was recruited by S.H.I.E.L.D., where he met Natasha. Natasha was a Russian super-spy trained in martial arts.

Ultimately, they became known as the Super Heroes Black Widow and Hawkeye.

Meanwhile, on a highly classified military base, Dr. Bruce Banner was hard at work. An Army scientist who studied gamma radiation, Bruce was always a mild-mannered man. But one day, Bruce was accidentally hit by stray gamma rays. After that, Bruce had some trouble controlling his temper. . . .

"Oh no, not again!" Bruce said after breaking a beaker. Whenever Bruce became angry or afraid, he would transform into a big, green Super Hero known as the Hulk!

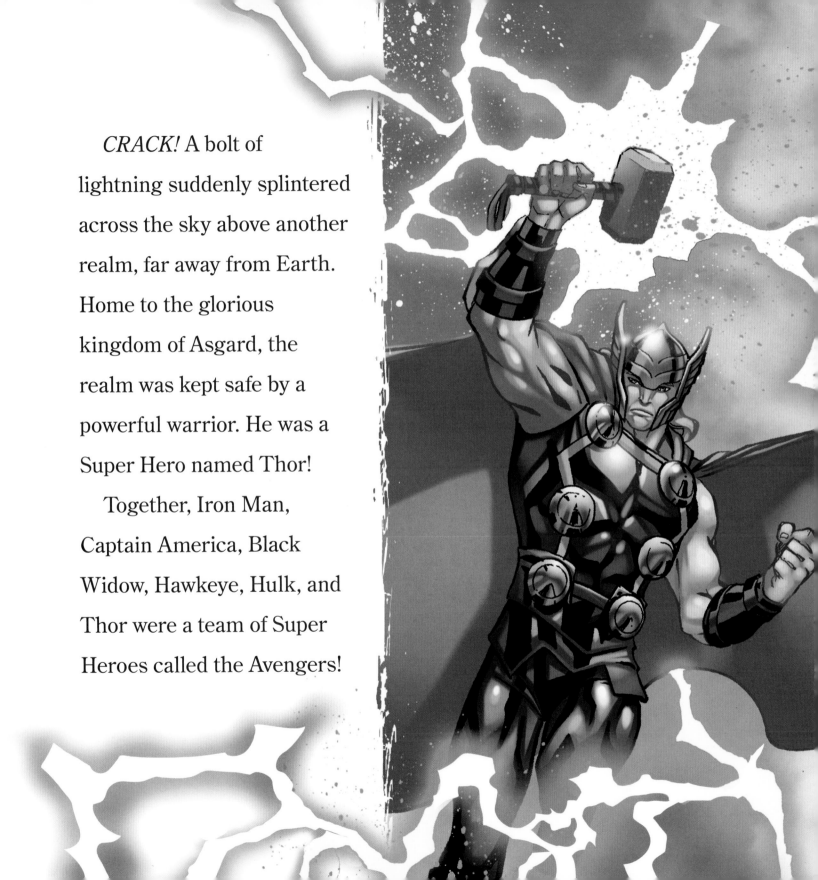

CRACK! A bolt of lightning suddenly splintered across the sky above another realm, far away from Earth. Home to the glorious kingdom of Asgard, the realm was kept safe by a powerful warrior. He was a Super Hero named Thor!

Together, Iron Man, Captain America, Black Widow, Hawkeye, Hulk, and Thor were a team of Super Heroes called the Avengers!

Thor had a brother, named Loki. Growing up, Loki had always been jealous of Thor. As the first born, Thor would rule Asgard one day, and this made Loki angry. While his brother trained to be a hero, Loki learned the dark arts.

Thor and Loki would battle constantly, but Thor would always win.

Although Thor was honor-bound to protect Asgard, he had a soft spot in his heart for Earth. He liked humans and felt they needed his protection, too. Using the Bifröst Bridge, Thor could travel anywhere in the Nine Realms. One day, he traveled to Earth on the bridge to join his fellow Super Heroes. But Thor didn't know that Loki had followed him!

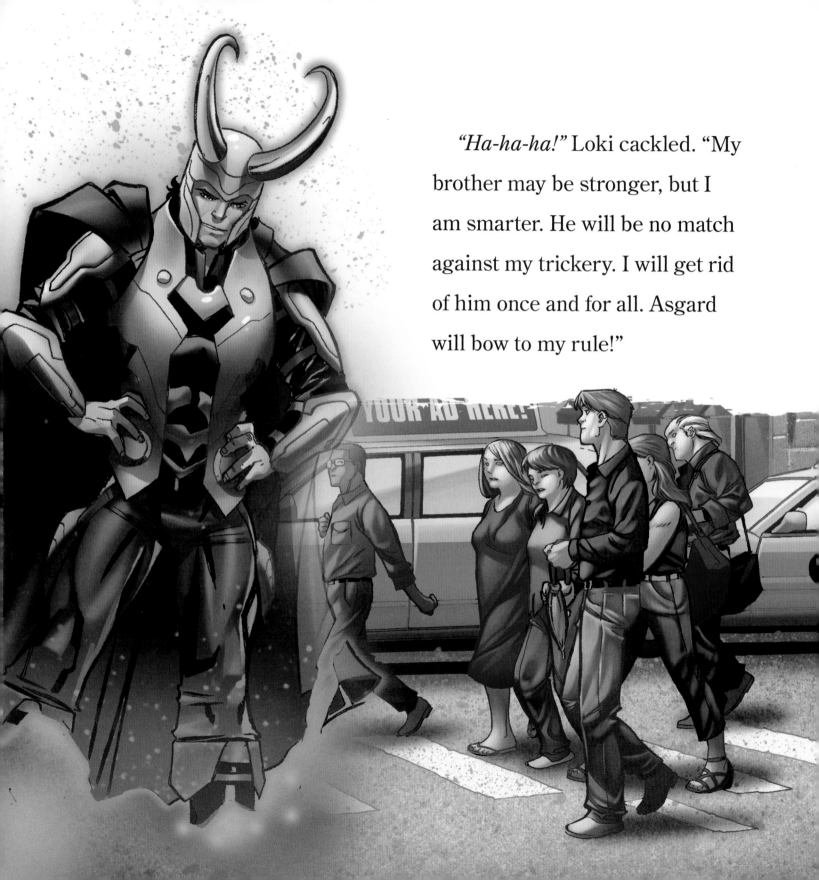

"Ha-ha-ha!" Loki cackled. "My brother may be stronger, but I am smarter. He will be no match against my trickery. I will get rid of him once and for all. Asgard will bow to my rule!"

Loki knew Thor was too strong to defeat on his own. So, he used his dark, magical powers to search the universe for someone fearsome enough to destroy Thor. Eventually he found himself on Earth.

"Earth? Yuck. I have no idea why my brother frequents this place," Loki said, looking out on a street full of people. "The only redeeming quality is that big green— Wait. Now there's an idea!"

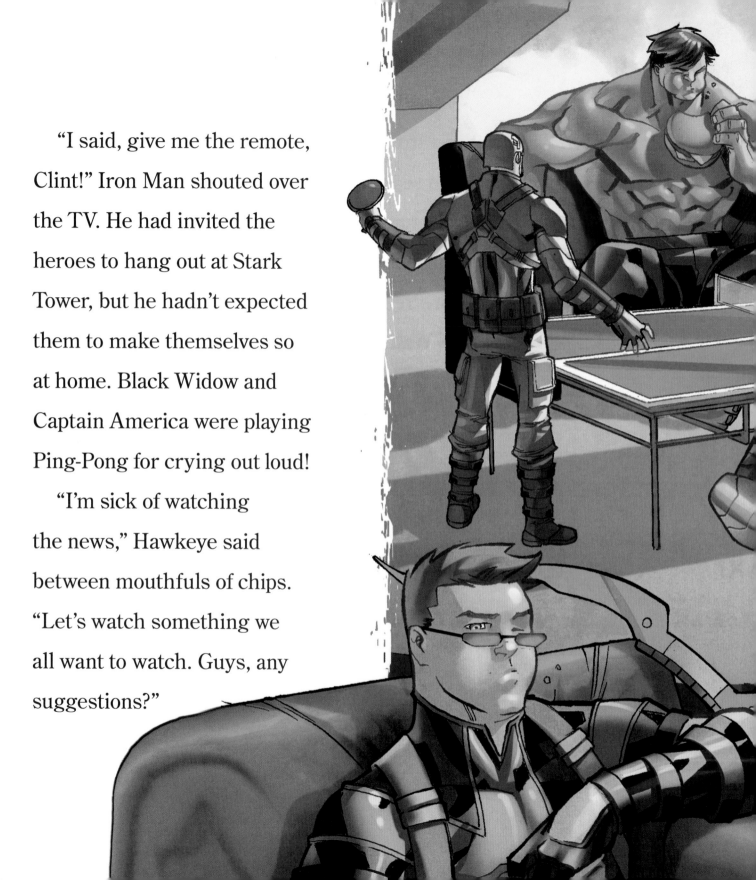

"I said, give me the remote, Clint!" Iron Man shouted over the TV. He had invited the heroes to hang out at Stark Tower, but he hadn't expected them to make themselves so at home. Black Widow and Captain America were playing Ping-Pong for crying out loud!

"I'm sick of watching the news," Hawkeye said between mouthfuls of chips. "Let's watch something we all want to watch. Guys, any suggestions?"

Hulk snorted as he ate a massive cheeseburger. "Hulk want to watch football. Go—!"

Suddenly Hulk noticed something move out of the corner of his eye. Warily, he continued to munch on his cheeseburger.

Loki slowly shimmered back into view outside the window of Stark Tower. He had almost been spotted by Hulk! Relieved, he concocted his evil plan. "I just need to influence this Hulk creature," he whispered, "and then Thor won't know what hit him!"

Silently, Loki shimmered into Stark Tower and stood right behind Hulk. Using the full force of his powers, Loki began to say things inside Hulk's mind!

"You are a monster, Dr. Banner," Loki taunted. "No amount of heroism will change that. You are a hideous beast. These humans will never accept you. Destroy them ALL!"

Loki's words made Hulk *angry*. In a blind rage, Hulk ran out of Stark Tower. Shocked by their friend's sudden rampage, the Avengers quickly tried to follow him. But Hulk was too fast!

Loki guided Hulk to a small town outside the city, where he did the most damage. He slammed his fist into a house, completely leveling it!

Loki's trick had worked! He looked out on the town in the wake of Hulk's destruction. A crumbling house was burning in the distance. Loki gave an evil grin. He was ready for the battle to come.

"My brother will have no choice but to save this sad little town from his friend's temper tantrum. And when he comes, Thor will be no match against Hulk. My brother will be destroyed, if it's the last thing I do!"

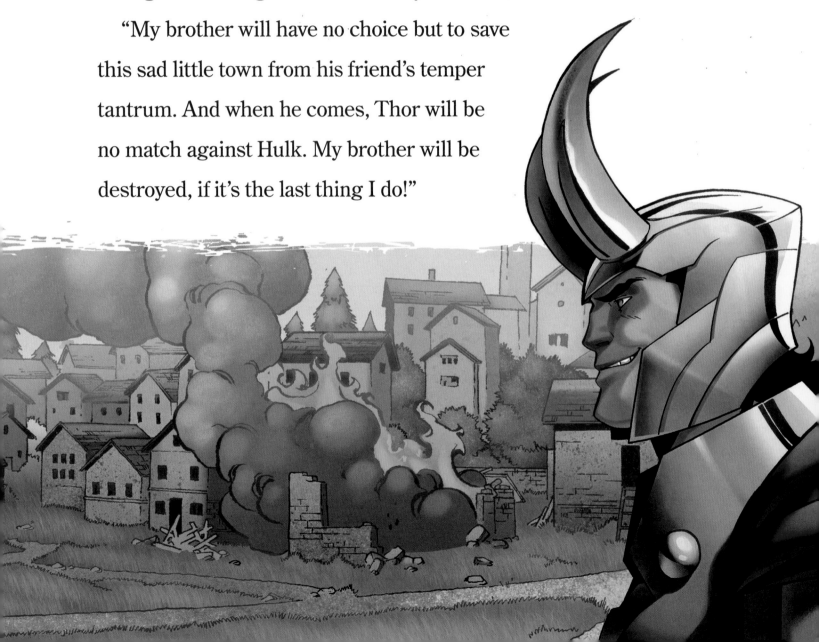

Avengers Assemble!
Part Two

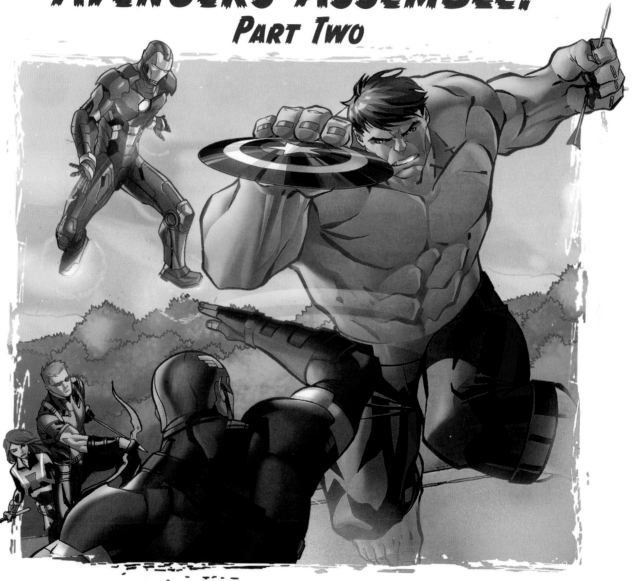

"**A**VENGERS, ASSEMBLE!" Captain America shouted as they followed Hulk's path of destruction. Very soon, Captain America, Iron Man, Black Widow, and Hawkeye arrived on the scene. Police officers were already there trying to protect civilians. Captain America helped Black Widow and Hawkeye clear the crowd away.

Suddenly the sky was filled with thunder and lightning. "I heard there was some trouble afoot," Thor's voice boomed.

Loki cackled in Hulk's head. "*Ha-ha-ha!* My plan is working! My silly brother has come to defeat the threat. Little does he know, this battle will be his last."

Hulk *roared* in anger.

"Nice of you to join us, Thor," Iron Man said. "Here's the deal. Something has gotten into Hulk. We don't want to hurt him, but we need to calm him down."

"Got it," Thor replied. "But this is your comrade. You take the lead and I'll follow."

The Avengers had to stop Hulk before he did any more damage. Captain America threw his shield and Hawkeye shot one of his arrows at Hulk. But Hulk simply caught them both in his hands. At the same time, Black Widow tried to calm Hulk down, but he became defensive. He lashed out, sending her flying through the air and knocking her into Hawkeye.

"Take a chill pill, big guy!" Iron Man said. "Nobody has to get hurt."

"They're trying to destroy you," Loki whispered in Hulk's mind. "You *are* the monster!"

Somehow Hulk became even angrier. He hurled both Captain America's shield and Hawkeye's arrow at Iron Man, who leaped out of the way just in time.

"Hulk," Thor said. "Snap out of this madness!"

Hulk roared and charged toward Thor, who quickly jumped out of the way. But Hulk was unfazed and charged again. This time, Thor sidestepped the charge and swung his hammer low to trip the green Avenger. Hulk went crashing to the ground! But he just shook his head and got right back up.

"I'm running out of nonviolent options!" Thor cried out to the heroes.

Thor did not want to hurt Hulk, but he had to protect himself. He swung his hammer at the giant, who roared in a blind rage. Hulk was no longer in control. He was focused on only one thing. *Smash!*

Loki's trick was going to work even better than he expected. Not only would he finally defeat his brother, Thor, but he would also see these Super Heroes destroy each other in the process!

"We may need some help controlling this beast!" Thor shouted.

With that, Thor threw his hammer straight into Hulk's stomach, landing one massive blow. Hulk doubled over, fuming. His rage grew, and grew, and grew.

"BEAST?!" he roared. "Hulk SMASH!"

"Nooo!" the heroes shouted in unison as Hulk picked up the Asgardian warrior. Hulk slammed him into the pavement, creating a small but powerful earthquake that vibrated throughout the world!

Seeing Thor defeated on the ground, Loki knew his moment of victory had come. He suddenly shimmered into view, lording over his brother triumphantly.

"Surprised to see me, dear brother?" Loki crowed.

Thor's eyes narrowed. "Loki! I should've known you had a hand in this mayhem."

"You so-called Avengers may be strong," Loki taunted, "but you're not very smart. It was almost too easy to trick you!"

That was all Hulk needed to hear. His rage turned toward Loki. "Hulk strong—and smart!" he yelled. He charged at Loki and smashed with all his might, sending the villain flying through the air.

But Loki had one more trick up his sleeve. He used his powers to create multiple illusions of himself, so that the heroes could not tell which Loki was the real one.

"This should make the battle a bit more interesting," Loki said. "Catch me if you can!"

But Hulk knew exactly what to do. He swung his arm in a wide arc, his fist going through each fake Loki until it hit the real one.

"No more tricks!" Hulk yelled.

He grabbed Loki's shoulders, lifted him up in the air, then brought him crashing to the ground.

"I agree," Thor said. "No more tricks. Your fun is over."

Loki had tried to turn the Avengers against one another, but he had only made the Super Hero team stronger.

"Let's take this guy back to S.H.I.E.L.D. and let them deal with him properly," Captain America said.

"Yeah," Hawkeye agreed. "No offense, Thor, but your brother is really annoying."

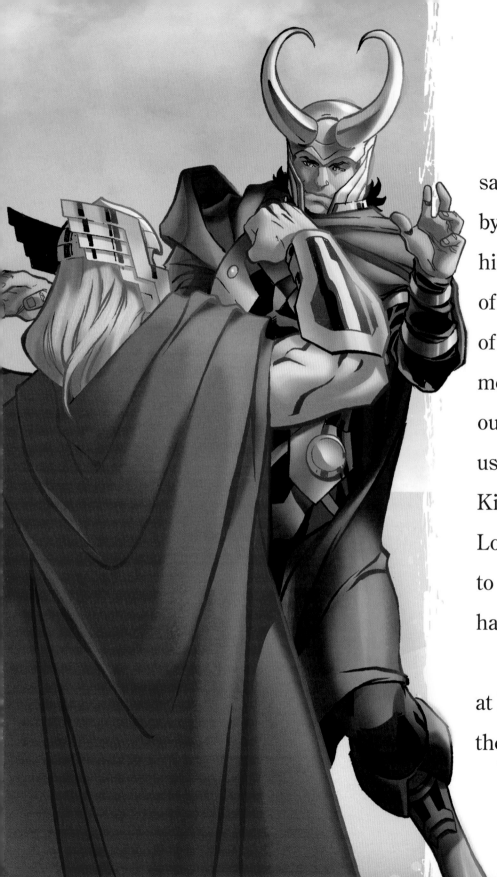

"You're right," Thor said, grabbing his brother by the cape and hoisting him into the air. "But all of this happened because of Loki's grudge against me. We are brothers, but our differences have made us enemies. As the future King of Asgard, I must take Loki back to my kingdom to stand trial for what he has done."

Captain America looked at his fellow heroes and then nodded. "Very well."

On Asgard, Thor locked Loki in an underground chamber of the palace. "You've caused enough trouble for one lifetime," he said.

"Why do you waste your time with such foolish mortals?" Loki sneered, gripping the bars of his jail cell.

"You are the foolish one," Thor replied. "Those heroes have more courage and compassion than you'll ever know."

A while later, Thor flew back to Stark Tower to apologize to his fellow Avengers. "I am sorry for my brother's mischief," he said.

Hulk smiled, accepting the apology, while Iron Man just shrugged. "Brothers can be like that sometimes. But we're missing the bigger picture here. I've redecorated! Welcome to the all-new AVENGERS Tower."

The Avengers smiled, because Earth's Mightiest Heroes were home.

The Doom of Fin Fang Foom!

A **BOLT OF LIGHTNING** cracked across the sky as Thor landed on top of Avengers Tower. He had just defeated the Enchantress, and was looking forward to regaling his fellow Avengers with stories of his epic triumph.

"Hulk! Captain America!" Thor boomed as he walked into the training room. "Come hear about my latest conquest."

Captain America and Hulk rolled their eyes. Being friends with Thor was great, but the guy could be really bigheaded sometimes.

"Hulk, come here and let me show you how I did it," Thor said. Hulk reluctantly walked over. "There's my colossal comrade!"

Suddenly Thor used his hammer to put Hulk in a headlock. "So, see what I'm doing here?" Thor said, encouragingly. "Cap! Are you watching?"

"Look, buddy," Captain America began, "don't be so rough with Hulk. He may be a green goliath, but he's still your friend."

"Hulk annoyed," Hulk said.

Thor wasn't really listening to what Captain America was saying. He didn't think he was being too rough with Hulk.

"You come back from these battles with a pretty big head," Cap continued. "Just be careful. Or one day you may find yourself in a major fight without any backup."

Thor was doubtful of his friend's advice. Shrugging his shoulders, Thor headed straight to the lab to look for Nick Fury. He was ready for his next mission. As Thor waited in the lab, he glanced at one of the glowing screens. Lazily, he touched one, and it suddenly slid down to reveal a tiny dragon! Thor examined the strange object. *Huh. Weird*, he thought as he set the figurine back onto the table.

With nothing else to do, Thor began to daydream. He thought back to his fight with the Enchantress. Thor stood up and began reenacting the battle.

Thor swung his hammer dramatically in the air. "Nice try, Enchantress! Bow before Thor, son of—" Suddenly he heard a tiny *crack*. Thor had accidentally knocked over the dragon, breaking it in half! The room quickly began to fill with thick green smoke.

As the smoke cleared, Thor could see the room was destroyed and there was a massive hole in the side of the tower. But Thor wasn't worried about the hole. He was worried about the forty-four-foot-tall dragon monster that had just materialized!

"Who has awoken Fin Fang Foom from his slumber?!" the monster bellowed.

"Prepare to be defeated, beast!" Thor said, raising his hammer above his head.

"You dare challenge me?" Fin Fang Foom laughed. "I have wreaked havoc upon this planet before, and I will do it again. Over and over. Humanity will pay for the crimes they've committed against my kind!"

Fin Fang Foom smashed his massive hand against the crumbling wall of Avengers Tower. The entire building shook from the impact, throwing Thor off-balance. He steadied himself and attacked Fin Fang Foom with his mighty hammer. But the monster didn't even flinch.

"Ha-ha-ha! Nice try, puny warrior."

Hearing the commotion, Hulk and Captain America rushed into the lab. When they saw the monster, their mouths fell open.

Cap began to shout orders. "Hulk! Ready on my—!" But suddenly Fin Fang Foom landed one final blow to Thor. The monster turned to smile at the heroes. "Well, better be off. Things to do, planets to destroy." With that, he flew toward the city.

Thor looked back at his friends, his eyes dark with anger. "*Don't follow me.*"

Hulk looked at Captain America. "Need to help Thor."

"I know, buddy," Cap replied. "Come on! We need to hop on the Quinjet before it's too late."

The heroes quickly settled into the cockpit as Cap described his plan. "We need to get up in the air. We're looking for a giant dragon monster and an Asgardian warrior. How hard can it be?"

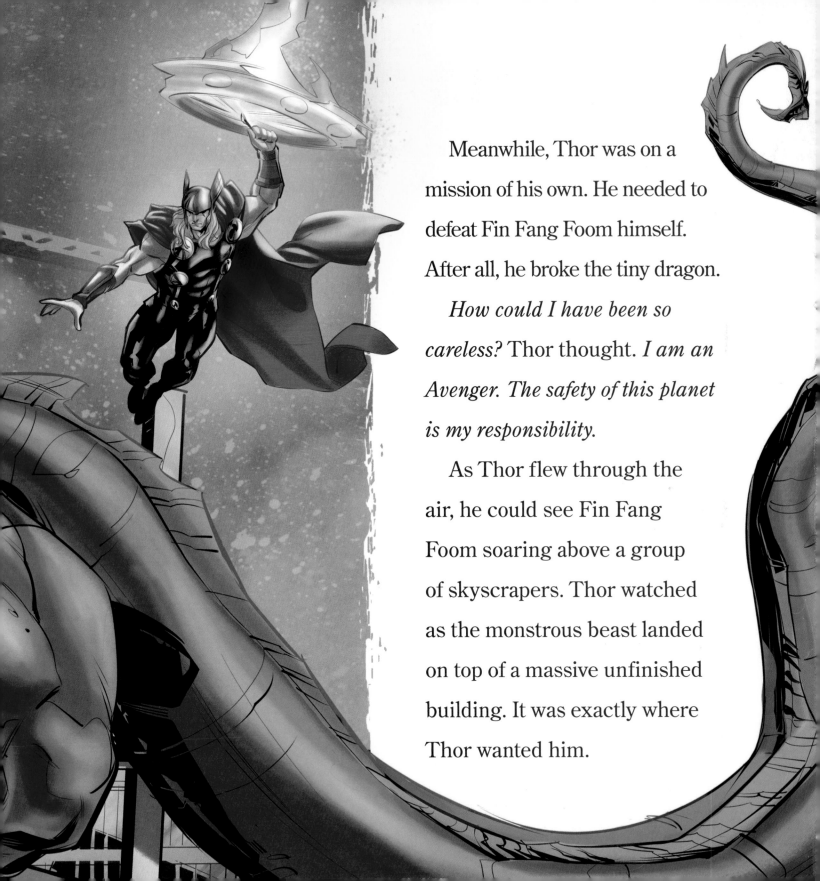

Meanwhile, Thor was on a mission of his own. He needed to defeat Fin Fang Foom himself. After all, he broke the tiny dragon.

How could I have been so careless? Thor thought. *I am an Avenger. The safety of this planet is my responsibility.*

As Thor flew through the air, he could see Fin Fang Foom soaring above a group of skyscrapers. Thor watched as the monstrous beast landed on top of a massive unfinished building. It was exactly where Thor wanted him.

Thor knew if he could knock out the monster, it would buy him some time to figure out how to send him back to where he came from. Thor dove straight for the powerful beast. Then, with one mighty lunge, Thor used his hammer to hit the beast right in the gut!

"You are like a child with your silly attempts at defeating me!" Fin Fang Foom roared. As if he were batting away a pesky fly, Fin Fang Foom smacked Thor with his giant hand. Thor went crashing to the ground—along with half the building!

"There," Hulk grunted, pointing to the growing cloud of smoke. The heroes landed the Quinjet and ran over to Thor. He wasn't moving, but soon they were able to rouse him.

"Brothers, I am— " Thor began, but Hulk cut him off.

"Save world now. Sorry later."

They were going to defeat this menace once and for all. Together.

Suddenly they saw Fin Fang Foom dart past. He was headed straight for the Brooklyn Bridge!

Captain America, Hulk, and Thor charged Fin Fang Foom as one mighty team.

The monster roared as he latched on to the bridge, rocking it back and forth. "You will regret the day you ever messed with the great, the powerful . . . Fin Fang Foom!"

Suddenly Thor had an idea. "We must entrap the monster! Hulk, do what you do best!"

"HULK SMASH!" Hulk shouted as he pummeled the beast, sending Fin Fang Foom crashing into the water below the bridge. All seemed quiet, until the heroes heard a deep laugh from below. "*Ha-ha-ha!* You think a little water can trap me?"

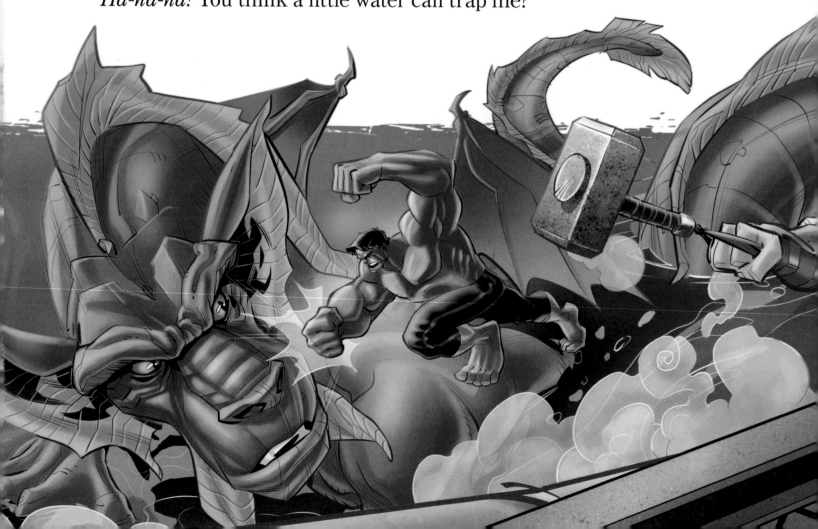

"No, but this might," Cap said as he produced the broken dragon from his pack. When he brought the two pieces together, the monster screamed in pain.

"Nooooo!" Fin Fang Foom cried as his massive body disappeared into a cloud of thick green smoke. Like that, he was absorbed back into the dragon, repairing it completely. The monster was back where he belonged.

Thor turned to his friends. "Fellow warriors, I apologize for my unseemly arrogance. I should have listened to you."

"You're an Avenger," Cap said after he put the tiny dragon safely into his pack. "We're family. But sometimes family can be annoying. Like, very annoying. Extremely—"

"Okay! I get it," Thor said.

"Back to training room?" Hulk asked. "Hulk bet he can SMASH puny Thor."

Thor smiled. "Verily!"

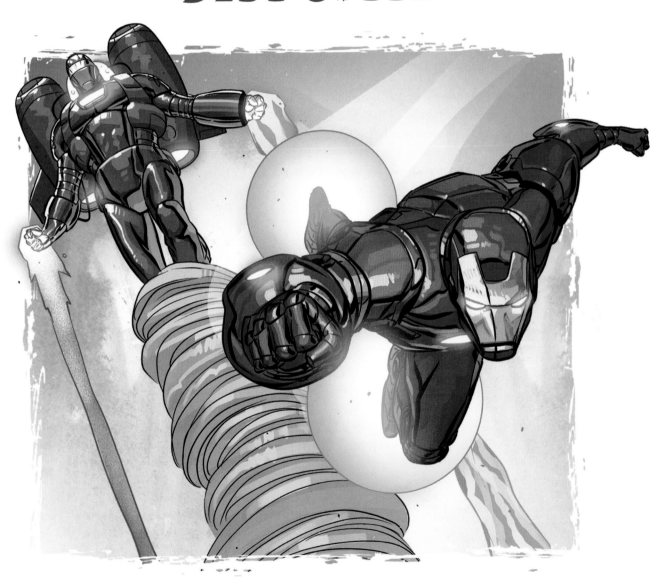

IF THERE WAS ONE THING Tony Stark loved, it was inventing new gadgets. "Just a few more tweaks," Tony muttered to himself, "and I will be— Oh, wait, what's this?" An image of chaos and panic flashed across his screens. A train station in the city was under attack!

"Guess this will have to wait until later," Tony said, rushing to put on his Iron Man armor. When he first made the suit, it took forever to put on. Now, the individual pieces of armor automatically flew to his body as he hurried to save the day.

"Come on, helmet, don't be late!"

On the other side of town, men and women scattered in fear as one of the trains lurched and careened off its track, coming close to slamming into some passengers.

Iron Man arrived just in time to pluck a commuter out of the way. Then he saw the villain who was causing all the commotion.

Iron Man's eyes narrowed as he confronted the familiar villain. "I didn't realize there was a Cyclone in today's weather forecast."

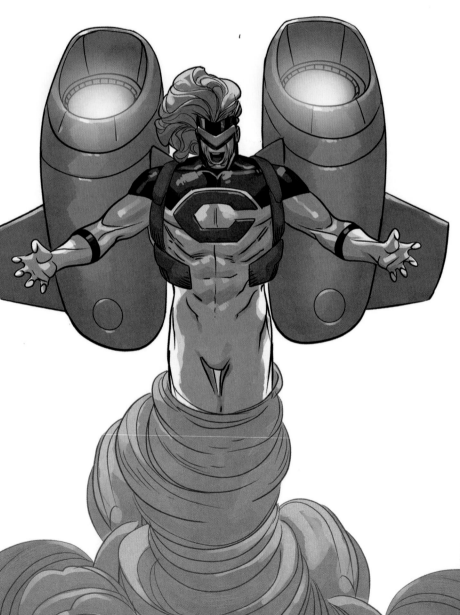

"Not just any Cyclone," the villain replied. "I'm a Category Five!"

He whipped up a funnel of wind and launched a

train car toward Iron Man.

Acting quickly, Iron Man flew up and intercepted the train car before it smashed into the crowd of innocent commuters. Then he guided it back down to the track.

"Category Five, huh?" Iron Man said. "Wouldn't have anything to do with those jet thrusters on your back, would it?"

"Are you jealous?" Cyclone taunted.

"Of those hunks of junk? Think again," Iron Man replied. "Besides, I bet I can still outfly you any day."

The villain smirked as his jetpack began to whir even louder and the winds grew even stronger. "We'll see about that!"

Iron Man knew he needed to disable Cyclone's jetpack before the villain created a full-blown hurricane.

"Say, did you ask the salesman if your jets can handle an electro-magnetic pulse?" Iron Man shouted over the wind.

"A what?" Cyclone replied.

"Never mind, let's just test it out," Iron Man said, activating an EMP in his own armor. The magnetic waves quickly fanned out and promptly disabled the thrusters in Cyclone's jetpack.

"WHOAAAAA!" Cyclone cried as he sputtered and spun out of control. Iron Man knocked the villain unconscious just as the wind finally died down.

Back in his lab, Tony Stark had time to examine Cyclone's jetpack more closely.

"This is pretty intense technology," Tony noted. "How did Cyclone get his hands on something like this?"

As he continued to tinker, Tony suddenly realized where he recognized the technology from: "This has to be the work of A.I.M. scientists!"

A.I.M.—or Advanced Idea Mechanics—was a group of brilliant scientists whose goal was to use technology to create disorder and chaos. If they were selling weapons and technology to the likes of Cyclone, that could only mean trouble.

"I've got to stop them," Tony said, "and I think I know how."

"If those A.I.M. goons think it's funny to give Cyclone all that extra horsepower, how about I give them a taste of their own medicine?"

Tony activated one of his autonomous battle robots and mounted Cyclone's jetpack on its back. Then he installed a propeller on the base so that it would create a small whirlwind as it flew—just like Cyclone!

Tony put on his Iron Man suit and took off for the A.I.M. research facility with his new invention. "Time to throw a wrench in their operation. Come on, let's go . . . Blue Crew? Blue Dude? Uhhhh, we'll figure it out later."

The A.I.M. research facility was well guarded, but Iron Man had a plan.

One of the guards spotted him. "Look! It's Iron Man and . . . what is that?!" he said.

"Hello, boys," Iron Man said confidently. "How's the weather down there?" Suddenly both Iron Man and his new invention *blasted* the guards. Not only had he given his new invention Cyclone's jetpack—he had also given him super-powered water guns!

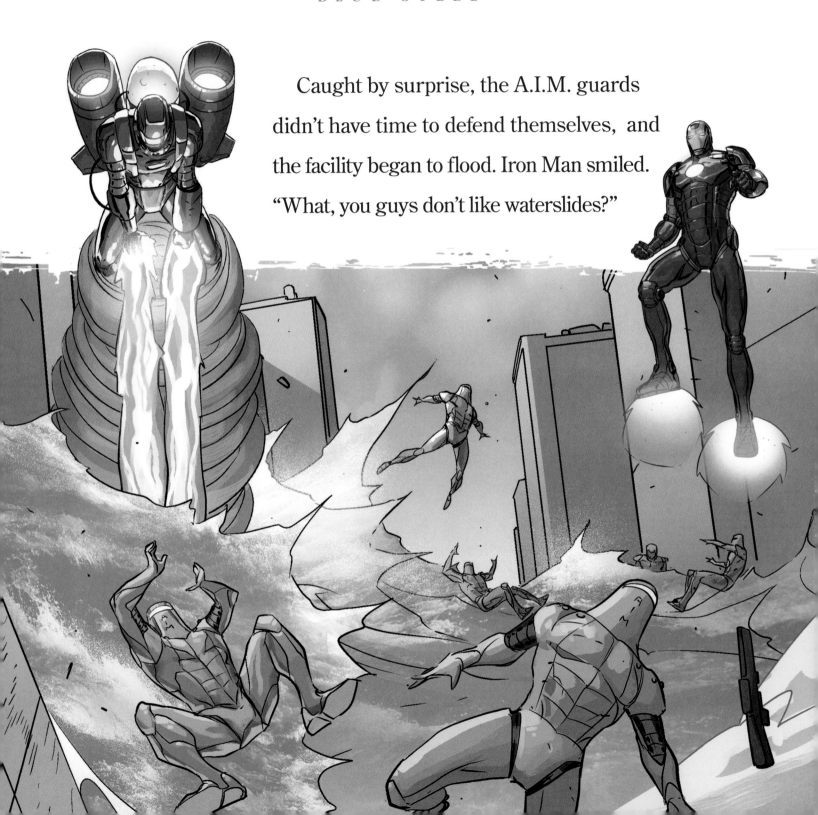

Caught by surprise, the A.I.M. guards didn't have time to defend themselves, and the facility began to flood. Iron Man smiled. "What, you guys don't like waterslides?"

Iron Man's plan had worked!

"See, this is what happens when you sell dangerous technology to people," Iron Man said. "Like karma, it always comes back around."

"You won't get away with this, Iron Man," the A.I.M. leader said.

"Actually, I already have," Iron Man replied. "Oh, and by the way, I'm keeping the jetpack. I need Blue Steel for my next pool party."

SHE-HULK SMASH!

"**ORDER IN THE COURT!**" the judge shouted, slamming his gavel down. The courtroom had erupted in a chorus of angry whispers as Ravage's cage was brought in. Ravage, once known as Professor Crawford, was standing trial for his crimes. He used Dr. Bruce Banner's gamma-radiated DNA to transform himself into a Hulk-like beast. But this beast was evil.

Just then, Ravage's lawyer, Jennifer Walters, stood up.

"How can you defend him?" Bruce whispered from behind her. She frowned. "Everyone deserves a fair trial. Even monsters."

Jennifer knew a thing or two about monsters.

Jennifer was Bruce's cousin. Bruce had used his DNA to save her life. It also gave her super-powers. When she's not defending the innocent as Jennifer, she's fighting villains as the Super Hero She-Hulk!

Just before Jennifer could begin to speak, Ravage's horrible roar filled the room.

"Get out of Ravage's head!" he shouted, gripping the metal bars with his massive fists. He pulled and pulled until he bent the bars, releasing himself from his prison. Then he roared again as he smashed through the courtroom wall and jumped down to the city below.

"Time to get angry," Bruce Banner whispered to himself. His body began to tremble as his skin turned bright green and his muscles *ripped* through his clothes. He had transformed into the Hulk!

Chasing after Ravage, Hulk landed with a massive thud on top of the crumbling asphalt. His breathing was heavy as he tried to focus his mind on finding Ravage. Hulk knew firsthand the damage a monster like Ravage was capable of.

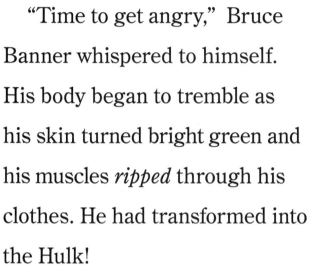

"Bruce, stop! Let me handle this," Jennifer shouted after her cousin. "Don't hurt him!"

Quickly changing into her suit, Jennifer Walters transformed into She-Hulk. Leaping out into the city, she knew she needed to find both Hulk and Ravage before anyone got hurt. But as She-Hulk flew through the air, she saw something very strange. It was the mysterious figure of a woman below, who was also following Hulk!

She-Hulk narrowed her eyes. "Hey, lady, or whoever you are! Come back here!"

When She-Hulk finally caught up to Hulk, they both confronted the strange woman.

"Hello, lovely creatures," the woman said in a singsong voice. "I am Mercy, and I've come to help you. Please, come with me."

She-Hulk scowled. "No thanks."

Mercy's sweet smile slowly transformed into a terrifying grin. Then she unleashed a powerful blast, knocking back both heroes!

Hulk quickly got to his feet and turned to Mercy. His entire body trembled with anger. "Mercy hurt She-Hulk! Hulk hurt Mercy!" He barreled toward the tiny villain, but she swiftly stepped out of the way. Hulk ran right into a brick wall.

"How lovely!" Mercy said, softly clapping her hands together. "Did you know that your anger feeds my powers? The angrier you get, the

stronger I become!" Mercy continued. "Oh, but please, I just want to help you. I have the power to help you sleep for all of eternity!"

Hulk continued to try and deflect Mercy's blasts, but her blasts just grew more powerful. They were starting to really take a toll on the hero.

"She-Hulk!" Hulk cried out. "Hulk need help!"

"Back off, lady!" She-Hulk shouted, grabbing Mercy and flinging her down onto the asphalt. The street cracked and crumbled under the enormous force as Mercy landed in a pile of rubble.

"Oh, ouch!" Mercy cried. "You may have defeated me, She-Hulk, but I still control the mind of your little friend. Ravage has so much anger. Isn't it lovely?"

Hulk and She-Hulk looked at each other, both realizing what had happened to Ravage. He became enraged in the courtroom because his mind was being controlled by Mercy!

"Hulk, we need to find him, but we can't leave Mercy," She-Hulk said.

Hulk nodded. "She-Hulk stay here. Hulk find Ravage."

"Well, okay, but please be careful. Don't—" But before she could finish, Hulk had left to find Ravage.

Hulk stood above the city, searching the streets. He suddenly had the strange feeling that somebody was watching him. . . .

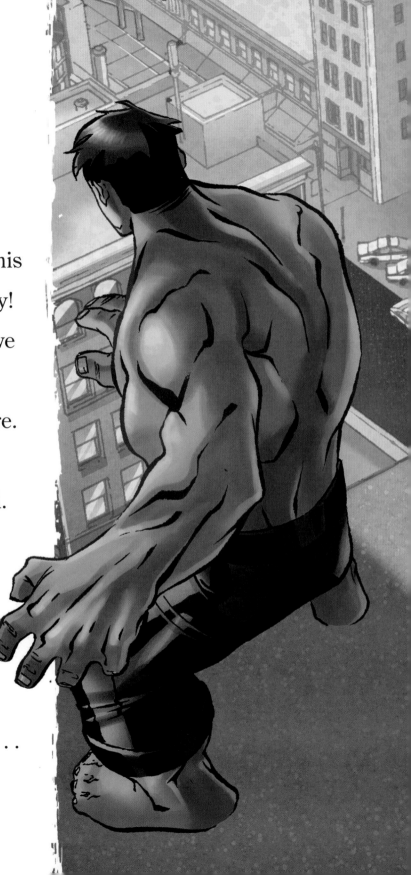

BOOM! Ravage threw his body on Hulk's and sent them both crashing into an abandoned building. They tumbled to the ground below, taking a chunk of the building with them. Hulk and Ravage roared in anger. The sound pierced the air, shaking the windows of every building in the city.

In the distance, She-Hulk heard her cousin's scream. "Bruce!"

As Hulk climbed out of the rubble, Ravage picked up a large slab of concrete over his head. "Ravage SMA—"

"UM, I don't think so!" She-Hulk said, cutting him off. The villain turned to see her standing behind him. She was ready to fight.

Hulk lifted his head weakly. "She-Hulk, no! Too dangerous."

But She-Hulk didn't listen. She *slammed* into Ravage, knocking him off-balance. He fell hard, dropping the slab of concrete.

"Mercy still has him under her control," She-Hulk said as she helped Hulk up while Ravage lay motionless on the ground. "We need to knock some sense into him. Literally."

But Ravage didn't stay motionless for long. He got up and seemed even angrier than before. If that was even possible.

"Ravage, stop!" She-Hulk shouted, lifting her hand as if to show him. "It's all in your head!"

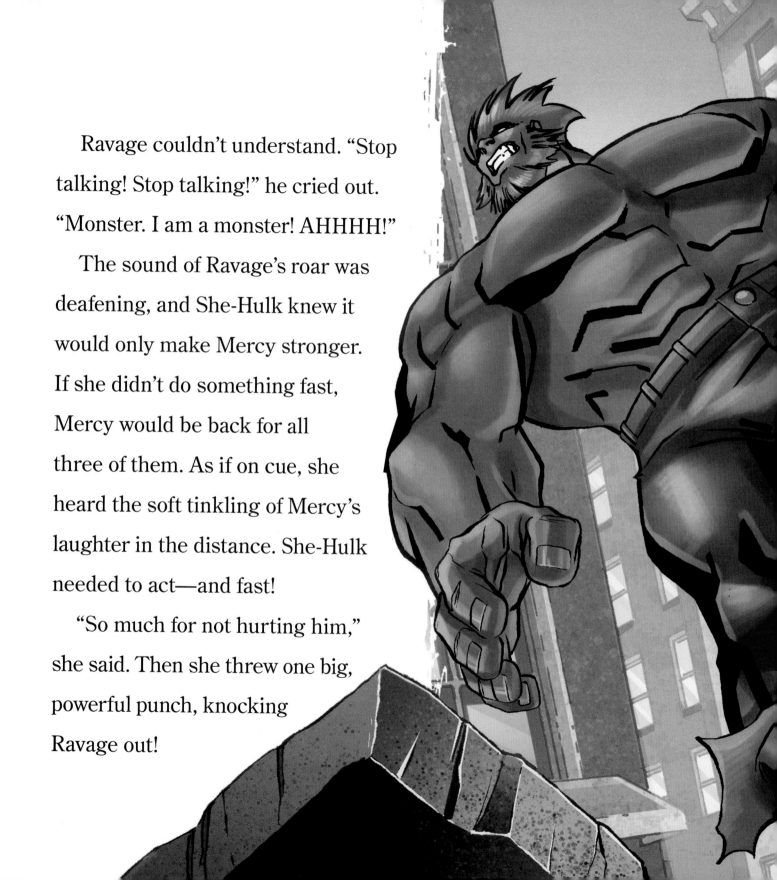

Ravage couldn't understand. "Stop talking! Stop talking!" he cried out. "Monster. I am a monster! AHHHH!"

The sound of Ravage's roar was deafening, and She-Hulk knew it would only make Mercy stronger. If she didn't do something fast, Mercy would be back for all three of them. As if on cue, she heard the soft tinkling of Mercy's laughter in the distance. She-Hulk needed to act—and fast!

"So much for not hurting him," she said. Then she threw one big, powerful punch, knocking Ravage out!

Back in the courtroom, the guards locked up the defeated Ravage in a special hi-tech cage. When She-Hulk knocked him out, it had cut the connection with Mercy. Without the link, Mercy had no anger to feed on and she mysteriously disappeared. Hulk had shrunk back down to the mild-mannered Bruce Banner, and She-Hulk had quickly changed back into her regular clothes. The trial proceeded as She-Hulk continued her defense. She worked hard to plead for Ravage's case. "He's not a monster," she said. "He's an innocent man in a monster's body."

After it was over, the judge read the sentencing. "I hereby find the defendant not guilty."

Bruce cheered. She-Hulk did it! The judge cleared his throat. "However, because of the damage caused, he will be handed over to S.H.I.E.L.D. for rehabilitation."

After Ravage was taken away, Bruce and She-Hulk left the courtroom together.

"Don't worry, cuz," Bruce said, trying to cheer her up. "He'll be fine. He just needs to learn to control his anger like I have."

"I know," she replied. "I just wish there was more I could do."

Bruce smiled. "Continue to fight for people like Ravage. Everybody could use a She-Hulk in their corner."

MARVEL AVENGERS
TRAINING DAY

"HAWKEYE, DUCK!"

Falcon shouted. Captain America's shield zipped over Hawkeye's head, just barely grazing his hair.

"Good looking out, Sam!" Hawkeye called back through gritted teeth. "These guys won't let up."

"Quick, head for the building!" Black Widow commanded.

"Oh, no you don't," Captain America shouted cheerfully. "You three are about to receive the best combat training in the world. If these S.H.I.E.L.D. agents and I don't have you whipped into shape before the day is over, I'll eat my hat."

"Geez, you really are old," Falcon said, following his fellow trainees inside the building.

Cap just smiled. He raised his voice even louder so they couldn't help but hear him. "In battle, you must always remember the four rules!"

"Rule number one," Captain America said, effortlessly catching his Vibranium shield as it bounced back to him. "Don't let the enemy out of your sight. If you let them slip away for even a moment, that's one moment longer you're giving them to figure out how to disarm you."

As he spoke, Cap locked eyes with two of his agents. He silently motioned for them to surround the building.

"This rule in particular is your greatest ally," Cap continued. "Without it, you're—"

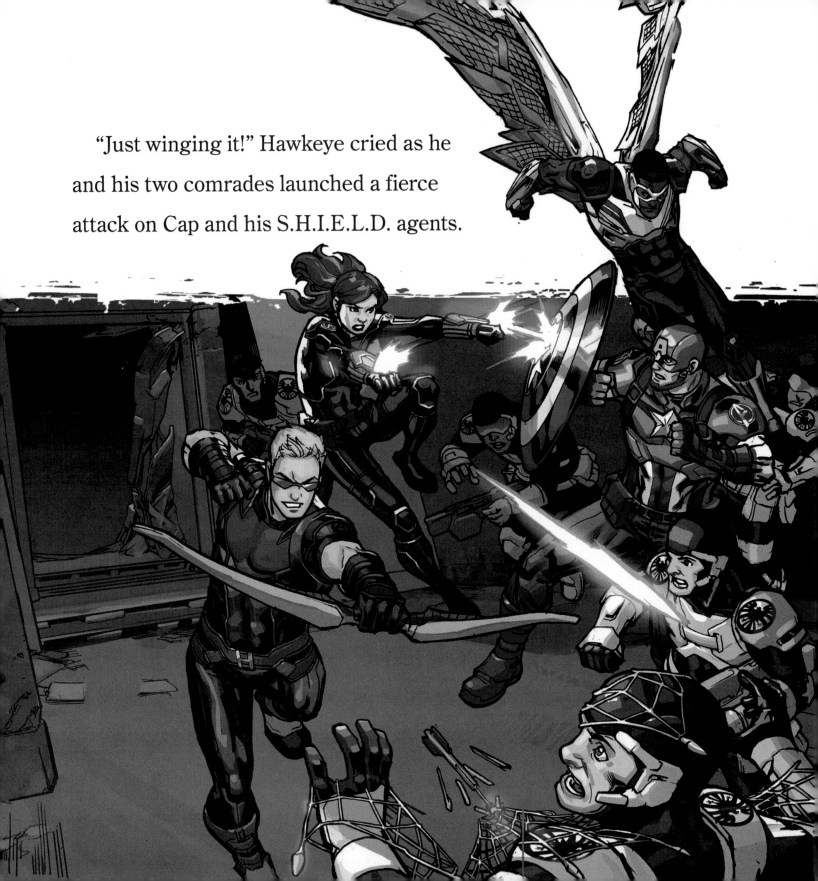

"Just winging it!" Hawkeye cried as he and his two comrades launched a fierce attack on Cap and his S.H.I.E.L.D. agents.

"Correct!" Captain America said, proudly. "Now, rule number two."

Using his superfast reflexes, Cap had managed to corner Falcon and Black Widow against a tree. The agents were focused on Hawkeye.

"Understand your enemy's strengths and weaknesses," Cap said. "See here, I understand that Black Widow and Hawkeye are a powerful pair. So I've divided them. And now I will conquer."

Black Widow smirked. "You think you're so smart!" She fired her Widow's Sting at Cap while Hawkeye shot flaming arrows.

While Captain America dodged Black Widow's blasts, Hawkeye and Falcon retreated into the upper branches of the tree. With one final *ZAP*, Black Widow managed to slip away. But the S.H.I.E.L.D. agents following close behind her.

"Hey, Cap!" Hawkeye called down. "So if Black Widow is my strength, then what's my weakness?"

Quick as lightning, Cap threw his shield straight at Hawkeye!

Caught off guard, Hawkeye tried reaching into his quiver. But he was forced to quickly block the strike with his steel bow. The Vibranium shield vibrated off the bow, clipping Falcon's wing. The powerful force knocked Falcon off-balance.

Captain America caught his shield in one hand, placing the other hand proudly on his hip. "Your weakness is pretty obvious. You always forget to count your arrows."

Meanwhile, Black Widow was having some fun of her own. In her jet-black suit, Black Widow could camouflage herself in any dark corner. Her unsuspecting enemy would hear only the faint whirring of her Widow's Sting.

As she hid in the shadows of the building, Black Widow patiently waited for her prey to fall into her trap. The lone S.H.I.E.L.D. agent just needed to come a little closer. . . .

Without a sound, Black Widow leaped gracefully from her hiding place. She wrapped her legs around the agent's neck and squeezed as tight as she could.

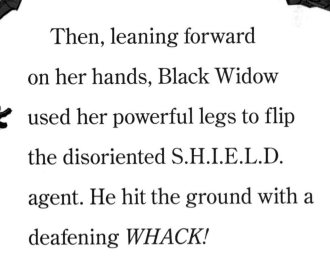

Then, leaning forward on her hands, Black Widow used her powerful legs to flip the disoriented S.H.I.E.L.D. agent. He hit the ground with a deafening *WHACK!*

Victorious, Black Widow turned to leave. But suddenly, a dangerous blast whizzed past her head. "Hey!" She turned to find the S.H.I.E.L.D. agent on his feet. His blaster was pointed directly at her. She raised her arms, her Widow's Sting whirring with power.

TAP! TAP! TAP! Black Widow felt a gentle knocking against the back of her head. It was Captain America and his shield. "Rule number three: confirm that your enemy is down. No one likes surprises."

"So let's review," Captain America said as he gathered up his defeated trainees. "Rule number one: don't let the enemy out of your sight. Rule number two: understand your enemy's strengths and weaknesses. Rule number three: confirm that your enemy is down."

"What's rule number four?" Falcon asked.

"Keep moving forward," Captain America said. "As a soldier, always try to push back the enemy line. As a hero, keep training and keep learning. You three are each uniquely skilled and the best in your field. But as a team? You're unstoppable."

As the heroes headed back to headquarters, Falcon waved to Cap. "Thanks for everything today, buddy. And you can bet that next time, we'll remember to D.U.C.K.!"

MARVEL Avengers
A Heroic Little Helper

"**STAR-LORD, ON YOUR LEFT!**" Iron Man shouted over the battle. Kree soldiers, warriors from a vengeful alien race, had launched an attack on the planet Xandar. The fighting was so fierce, the Guardians of the Galaxy had to call in reinforcements. Star-Lord frowned. "Just because I let you Avengers ride in the *Milano* doesn't mean you can boss me around!"

Xandar was in total chaos. Outnumbered, they tried to escape and regroup, but something was wrong. The *Milano* wouldn't start!

"We'll hold them off," Captain America said.

"Rocket, Groot, fix the ship. We need to leave pronto!"

"Okay, you heard the man," Rocket said. "I'll go check on the thrusters. You stay here and wait for my signal."

Groot gave a tiny salute. "I am Groot!"

Groot wasn't as big as he used to be, but he could still try to be a big help. All he had to do was focus and not get distracted. But that was hard to do when he noticed three tiny Orloni making their way onto the ship! If there was one thing Groot couldn't stand, it was Orloni. They were the sneakiest pests in the galaxy.

"RAWWWR!" With a fierce scream, Groot jumped toward the pests. But the Orloni scattered away just in time. Two of them ran behind some equipment against the wall, while the other ran toward the cargo hold. Groot set his jaw in determination and chased after the creature. No Orloni was going to cause mischief while he was around!

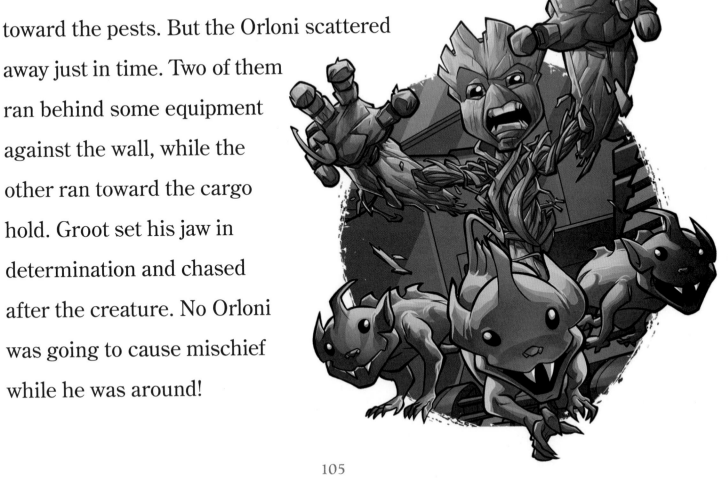

Groot rushed into the cargo hold and saw Iron Man crouched behind a box. He was firing at a Kree fighter who had made his way onto the ship. The Orloni was headed straight for Iron Man! Groot hurried after it, not paying attention as he knocked into a weapons rack holding Rocket's extra blasters.

One of the blasters fell, causing it to fire just as Iron Man ducked. *PEW!* The shot hit the Kree soldier, and he crashed against the wall.

"What's all the ruckus about?" Rocket asked, poking his head in from the engine room.

"Alien guy almost had me," Iron Man replied. "But tiny tree dude got him!"

Groot was surprised. "I am Groot?"

"Way to go, pal!" Rocket cheered.

Eyes wide, Groot looked over at the Kree soldier. Inside one of the fallen crates, Groot saw something move—it was the Orloni! It must have gotten trapped when the blast knocked out the soldier.

Groot beamed with pride. "I am Groot!"

"Nice fighting, little guy," Iron Man said. Groot waved good-bye as Iron Man quickly jumped back into the fight outside.

"Let's get back to work," Rocket said to Groot. "This planet is getting on my last nerve."

"I am Groot?" Groot asked.

"Yeah, yeah, I checked the lines," Rocket replied. "There isn't enough power getting to the thrusters. Let's go check what's blocking the pipes."

When the friends found the ship's main pipe, Groot suddenly had an idea. "I am Groot?"

But Rocket wasn't so sure. "I guess you're small enough to fit, but it's way too dangerous. One wrong move and you could blow up the whole ship."

Suddenly Groot saw something run past. The second Orloni! Groot ran after the Orloni as it scampered straight into the main pipe.

"Groot, no!" Rocket yelled. But Groot was determined. Up and through the pipe system he chased, until the Orloni screeched to a dead end. But it wasn't a dead end at all—it was a mass of old sludge clogging the pipes. The Orloni kept ramming into the sludge until it burst right through. Suddenly Groot felt a deep rumble and heard Rocket's voice calling through the pipes.

"You did it, buddy!"

Groot could feel the engine heating up as he turned around and hurried back toward the entrance. He took a wrong turn and almost got lost, but finally, he saw Rocket's face at the opening of the grate. Rocket caught Groot and called out to the other heroes. "Okay, we're set, now let's get outta here!"

In the cockpit, Star-Lord set the thrusters to full power, and the *Milano* took off with a jolt, dodging fire from the Kree army as it ascended into space.

"Great job back there, Rocket!" Captain America said. "You got the ship working just in time."

"Don't thank me," Rocket said, lifting Groot up. "Groot was the one who risked his life to unclog the engine."

"I am Groot," Groot said, beaming as the heroes cheered. He was happy that he had helped his friends, but he couldn't stop thinking about that one Orloni that got away. . . .

MARVEL AVENGERS
PINT-SIZE POWER

ZZZZAAAAP! "Aaand there goes the electricity," Ant-Man said. The tiny hero and his partner, the Wasp, were standing in their lab. Well, what was left of it.

"Someone broke all my stuff!" Wasp said, her eyes trying to adjust to the darkness. Ant-Man was quiet for a moment, then he ran to a glass cabinet, flinging it open. "It's gone! The growth serum we've been working on is gone."

Wasp frowned. "UGH! Can this day get any worse?"

Ant-Man laughed. "Yes. We need to use the database at Avengers Tower."

"It just got worse!" Wasp said. "I like them, but those guys think they're better than us. We might be tiny, but we still get it done. Up top!"

Wasp's hand hung in the air, waiting for a high five. But Ant-Man left her hanging and headed out toward Avengers Tower. There, the two heroes tested DNA samples. Ant-Man turned and pointed at the screen. "It's Scarlet Beetle! Let's go— Oh hey, guys."

"What's up?" Black Widow said. "Can we help?"

While Wasp was having a really bad day, Scarlet Beetle was out in the city having an awesome day! Being a giant radiation-mutated beetle was tough. So Scarlet Beetle thought it was high time he made himself some friends. "Now that I have these vials of growth serum, I shall create an entire army of insects!"

"Now if I were a bug, where would I be?" Scarlet Beetle wondered. "Duh! I am a bug. Let's see—I love darkness and trash . . . the subway!"

Scarlet Beetle took off into the subway and poured growth serum over a family of cockroaches. The cockroaches grew until they were human-size! People screamed in horror as the bugs spilled out onto the streets.

"We need to squash this Scarlet Beetle," Iron Man said. "Shouldn't be too hard. He's only a bug."

Wasp narrowed her eyes. "Don't underestimate him. He may be a big bug, but he's also—"

"Got it," Iron Man said, cutting Wasp off. "Let's go."

With that, Iron Man led the charge to find the Scarlet Beetle. Zooming through the air, he was suddenly attacked by a swarm of angry yellow jackets!

But these were not just *any* yellow jackets—they were human-size.

"Whoaaa!" Iron Man shouted as one of the giant bugs attacked him.

"Did you know that yellow jackets are part of the wasp family?" Wasp called out.

Iron Man was trying to push the giant yellow jacket off before its stinger could puncture his suit. "Cool fact! Now can you help me?"

Wasp smiled and, using her Wasp Sting, she stunned the yellow jackets.

Down on the ground, Hulk, Black Widow, Hawkeye, and Thor were dealing with a swarm of their own.

"He poured the growth serum on the insect exhibit at the Natural History Museum!" Black Widow radioed to the heroes. "We can't contain them!"

"Ew, ew, ew," Hawkeye chanted, firing off his arrows into the incoming army of caterpillars. "I hate bugs!"

Suddenly the heroes heard someone cackling. When they turned, they saw Scarlet Beetle leading the charge on the back of a giant mosquito!

"Silly heroes, you think you can destroy my army with brute strength?" Scarlet Beetle taunted. "Well, think again. Insects outnumber humans on this planet. My insects and I will rule the world!"

"Not today, tiny creature!" Thor shouted on the rooftop, hurling his mighty hammer at the villain. The hammer hit the mosquito, knocking off Scarlet Beetle. "Noooo!" he cried as he began to fall down, down, down toward the roof.

"Hulk!" Thor commanded, "Squish him!"

Hulk curled his massive fingers into two giant fists. He smiled as he watched Scarlet Beetle fall. But suddenly, the Scarlet Beetle used his tiny claws to catch himself on the ledge of the building.

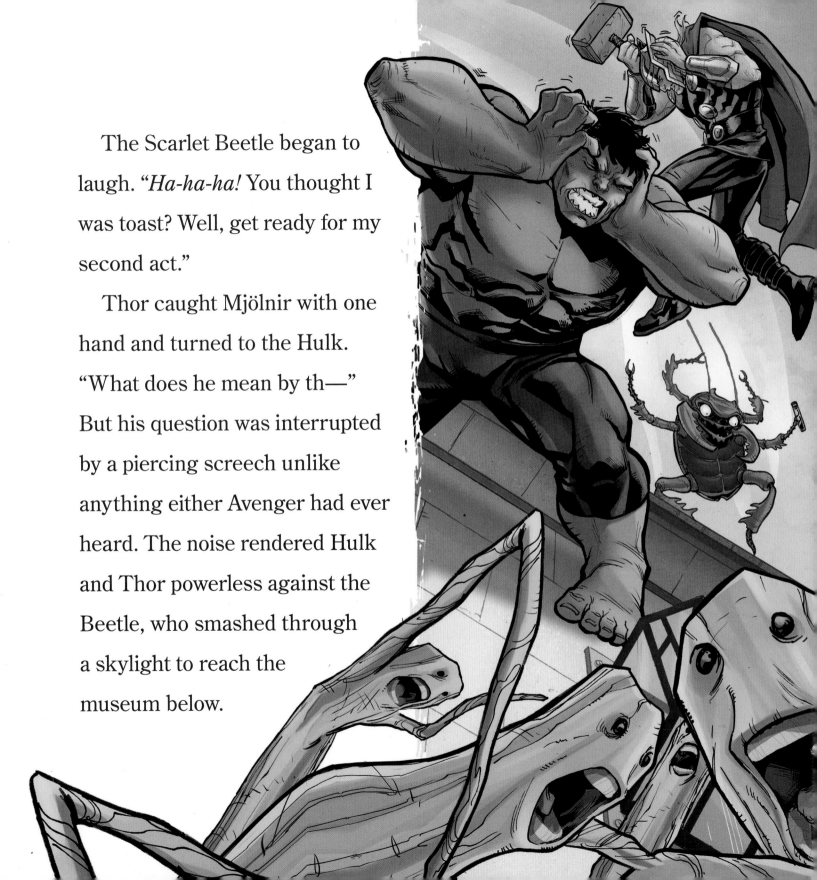

The Scarlet Beetle began to laugh. "*Ha-ha-ha!* You thought I was toast? Well, get ready for my second act."

Thor caught Mjölnir with one hand and turned to the Hulk. "What does he mean by th—" But his question was interrupted by a piercing screech unlike anything either Avenger had ever heard. The noise rendered Hulk and Thor powerless against the Beetle, who smashed through a skylight to reach the museum below.

Suddenly a strange mist appeared, covering everything.

"Stick bugs," Ant-Man explained as he zoomed by on his ant.

The mist was coming from the tiny gadget on his wrist. "They

disguise themselves as sticks to trick predators, and then use

sound to attack."

Thor threw up his hands, annoyed. "Earth creatures! So complicated."

Hulk rubbed his head. "Mist made bugs small."

"It's a new antidote I've been working on," Ant-Man said. "But I don't have enough to destroy an entire insect army."

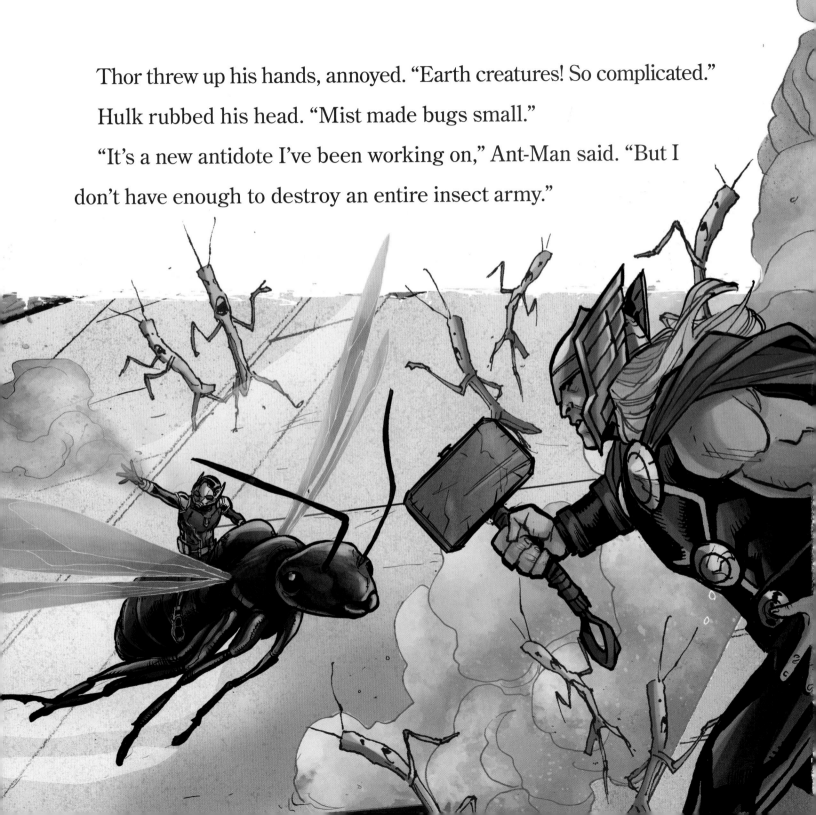

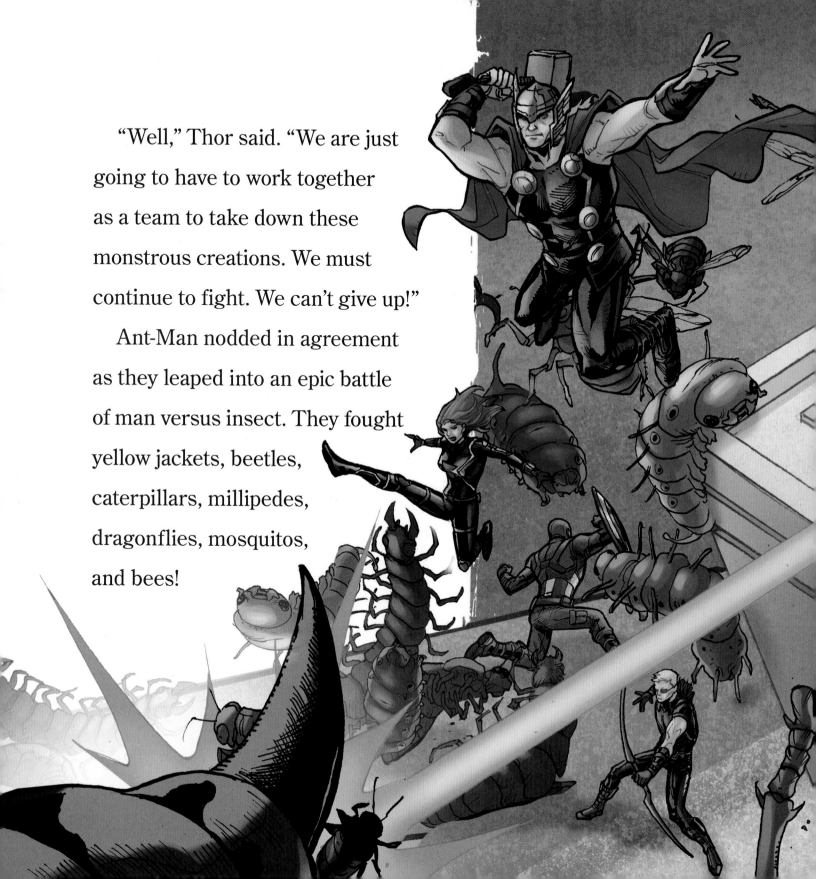

"Well," Thor said. "We are just going to have to work together as a team to take down these monstrous creations. We must continue to fight. We can't give up!"

Ant-Man nodded in agreement as they leaped into an epic battle of man versus insect. They fought yellow jackets, beetles, caterpillars, millipedes, dragonflies, mosquitos, and bees!

"Iron Man, aim for their wings, not their bodies!" Wasp commanded. "Their skeletons are on the outside."

"Thor!" Ant-Man shouted. "Stir up some thunder; the vibration calms them down!"

But the heroes didn't listen to Ant-Man and Wasp. They continued to fight with their fists and not their heads.

"Why aren't they listening to us?" Ant-Man cried out to Wasp, who was blasting away.

"I told you! They're too good for us bugs," she replied. "But I have an idea of how to get their attention. Avengers, ASSEMBLE!"

Suddenly every hero turned to look at Ant-Man and Wasp. They knew Wasp was serious and quickly huddled around the tiny heroes.

"There, that's better," Wasp said. "Now, here's the plan. Cap, Iron Man, and Black Widow, continue to keep the bugs at bay. Thor and Hawkeye, we need you. We only have a small amount of this antidote left and we need to make it count."

With their plan in place, the heroes leaped into action. The Scarlet Beetle had gathered his army of giant insects just as a sudden rain started falling.

"Nooooooo!" Scarlet Beetle cried as his insect army began to shrink. Suddenly Wasp smashed into him as Ant-Man soared in on Hawkeye's arrow. Grabbing the villain, the tiny heroes began to grow to full size and pulled him to the ground.

"It's over, Beetle. Thor's rainstorm is spreading the antidote," Ant-Man said as they landed.

"But I'm unaffected," the Scarlet Beetle mocked. "I shall end you two once and for all!"

"Are you sure there are only two of us?" Wasp asked. Suddenly the Beetle heard a deep voice from behind him. "Hulk SQUISH!"

"Hulk itchy," Hulk complained, when they finally got back to Avengers Tower. "Mosquito bites."

"Ant-Man and Wasp, you were amazing back there!" Captain America said. "We should have listened to you guys sooner."

"Oh, stop. . . . Okay, keep going," Wasp joked. Ant-Man smiled. "We're just glad that Scarlet Beetle is gone and there are no more human-size insects running around the city."

"Yeah," Iron Man said, exhausted. "Two is enough!"

Time Warp Teamwork

THE ENTIRE AVENGERS TOWER shook dramatically as the Avengers team practiced their combat training. Well, with one exception.

While Captain America, Thor, Hulk, Black Widow, and Hawkeye enjoyed spending hours in the training room, Tony Stark liked spending most of his time in the lab. Sometimes Tony felt very different from his fellow Avengers. They all had superhuman abilities. All Tony had was his Iron Man suit.

"What am I thinking?" Tony said. "I'm Tony Stark, for crying out loud! I'll just create something that's so amazing it'll change the Super Hero game."

Over the next few days, Tony worked on combining specific elements of his Stark tech to create a powerful new tool: a time machine! When the machine was ready for a test run, Tony suited up. He wasn't going anywhere unarmed.

"JARVIS," he commanded, stepping into the machine, "set time for 2099. Calculate crime ratios and synchronize the coordinates."

"Yes, Mr. Stark," JARVIS replied.

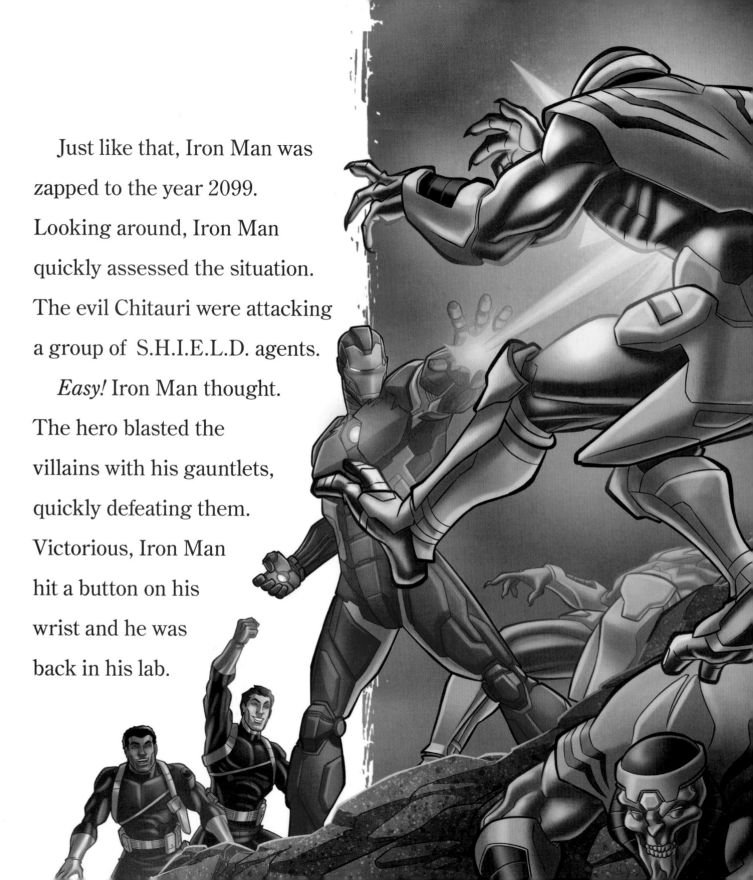

Just like that, Iron Man was zapped to the year 2099. Looking around, Iron Man quickly assessed the situation. The evil Chitauri were attacking a group of S.H.I.E.L.D. agents.

Easy! Iron Man thought. The hero blasted the villains with his gauntlets, quickly defeating them. Victorious, Iron Man hit a button on his wrist and he was back in his lab.

That afternoon, Iron Man revealed his new invention to the Avengers.

"We shouldn't take time travel lightly," Captain America said. "I would know. I was frozen for seventy years."

Iron Man's eyes narrowed. "I don't take saving the world lightly, old man."

Hawkeye smiled. "I'm willing to try it out."

"I love a new challenge," Black Widow added.

"Then it's settled," Iron Man said. "Prepare to be assigned your new missions."

"Black Widow and Hawkeye," JARVIS announced, "prepare to travel to 1840."

The pair were suddenly outside Buckingham Palace. Queen Victoria was riding by when Black Widow spotted a mysterious man trying to attack the queen! Using their stealth and speed, the heroes took down the attacker. Then, with the push of a button, they were back in the lab.

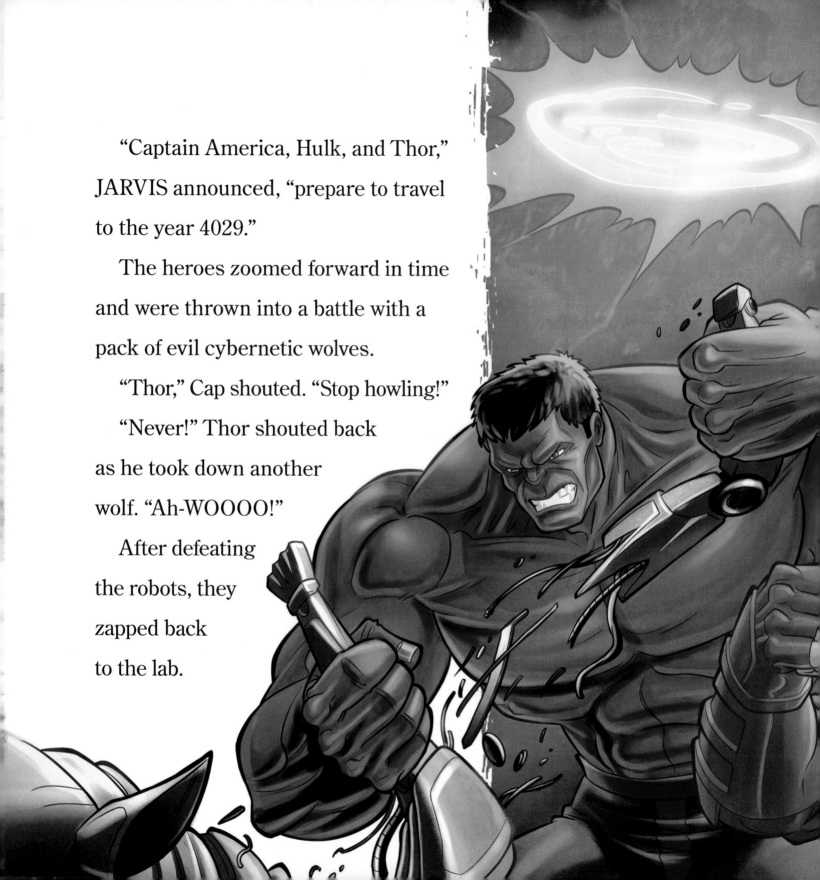

"Captain America, Hulk, and Thor," JARVIS announced, "prepare to travel to the year 4029."

The heroes zoomed forward in time and were thrown into a battle with a pack of evil cybernetic wolves.

"Thor," Cap shouted. "Stop howling!"

"Never!" Thor shouted back as he took down another wolf. "Ah-WOOOO!"

After defeating the robots, they zapped back to the lab.

The heroes did this all day, completing mission after mission.

"All right, JARVIS, give me a good one!" Iron Man shouted. The time machine rattled violently. Too violently. Then Iron Man was in the year 1792.

A masked man rounded the corner, using his blasters to destroy a local village. Iron Man smirked. "Easy."

Iron Man fired his repulsors, but the villain skillfully dodged the blasts. Annoyed, Iron Man stood right in the man's path. The masked rider charged. They both aimed their weapons and *fired*.

Iron Man opened his eyes. He was on the ground. He sat up and looked around. Then he saw the villain round the corner again. So Iron Man got up and stood in the man's path. They both aimed their weapons and fired. Again.

Iron Man opened his eyes. He was on the ground. He sat up and looked around. "Was I dreaming?" he said. "I'm having major déjà vu." Then he saw the masked man round the corner again. Iron Man kept trying to defeat the villain. But no matter how many times he tried, he kept getting hit.

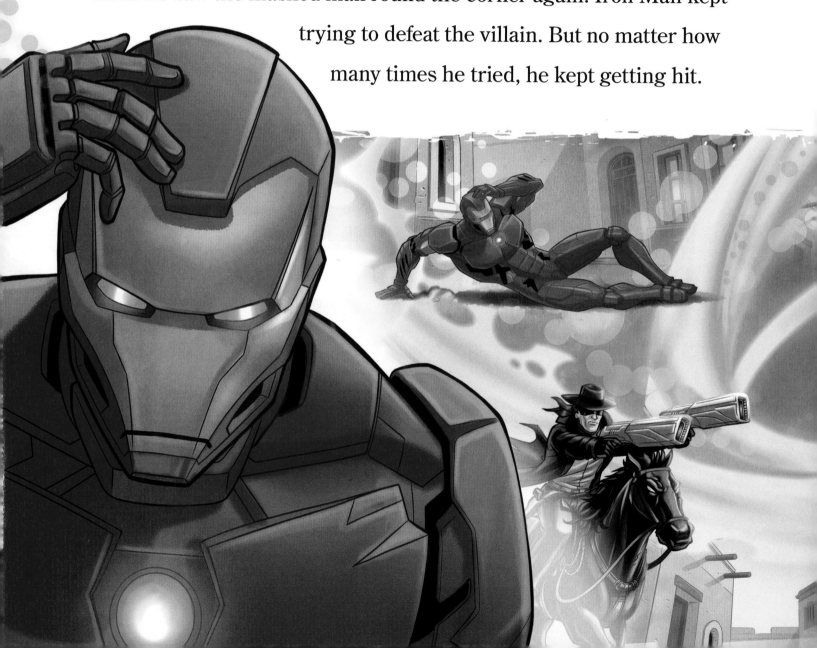

Iron Man opened his eyes. Again. He was on the ground. Again. He sat up and looked around. Again. Just like clockwork, the masked man rounded the corner. Again.

"This is impossible," Iron Man said to himself. "I'm stuck in a time loop."

Back in the lab, the Avengers were getting worried. Iron Man was missing and they had no idea where or *when* he could be.

"Look!" Black Widow said, holding up a schematic. "We just need to short-circuit the motherboard."

With that, Black Widow pointed her gauntlets at the machine, blasting the circuitry. Suddenly the portal opened.

Cap leaped into action. "I'm coming, buddy!"

The masked man was about to blast away Iron Man. Again! But Captain America jumped through the portal and flew in front of Iron Man just in time. He protected him with his Vibranium shield.

PEW! PEW! The blasts hit Cap's shield and bounced off.

"OOMPH!" the villain cried out in surprise. The powerful beams hit the man hard, knocking him off his horse.

"Finally," Iron Man said when he saw his teammates. "I thought I'd be stuck on repeat forever."

Captain America laughed as they quickly tied up the man. Suddenly the edges of the portal began to shimmer.

"Cap! Iron Man! Hurry or you'll be stuck!" Hawkeye shouted.

Cap's eyes widened with panic. "Come on, Tony, we need to get back to the present day!"

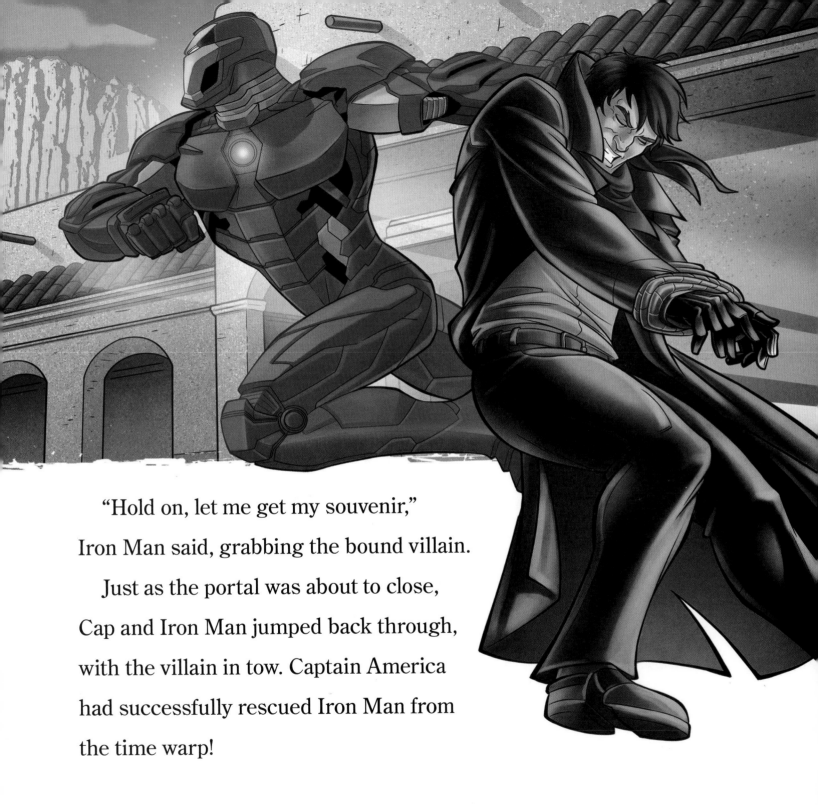

"Hold on, let me get my souvenir,"
Iron Man said, grabbing the bound villain.

Just as the portal was about to close,
Cap and Iron Man jumped back through,
with the villain in tow. Captain America
had successfully rescued Iron Man from
the time warp!

With the time machine broken beyond repair, the heroes sat around the lab recounting their time travel adventures. When it was his turn, Tony looked around at his friends.

"Thanks, everyone, for saving me back there," he said. "Especially you, Cap. You were right. Time travel isn't something to take lightly."

Cap put his arm around his friend. "Good advice. Even from an old man like me."

THE LEGEND OF BLACK PANTHER

THE LAND OF WAKANDA lay deep in the heart of Africa. It was a country born of great tribal traditions, owing much of its majestic beauty to the animals that inhabited its lands. Many years ago, an asteroid smashed into the Wakandan forest, delivering a massive amount of metal called Vibranium. With its unique ability to absorb vibration, Vibranium became extremely valuable.

As others learned about the Vibranium, Wakanda was often invaded by thieves and warriors. The Wakandan king recognized that his people needed a leader and a protector—a Black Panther! Fulfilling both roles, the Black Panther repelled invaders and protected Wakanda. When the threats grew too great, one king decided to close Wakanda's doors to outsiders. *Forever.*

Then a great Wakandan king named T'Chaka came along. T'Chaka inherited the Wakandan throne from his father. But a king does not inherit the title of Black Panther. He must earn the mantle through hard work, study, and training. When he finally earned his title, T'Chaka was beloved by his people. Under T'Chaka, Wakanda experienced decades of peace and prosperity.

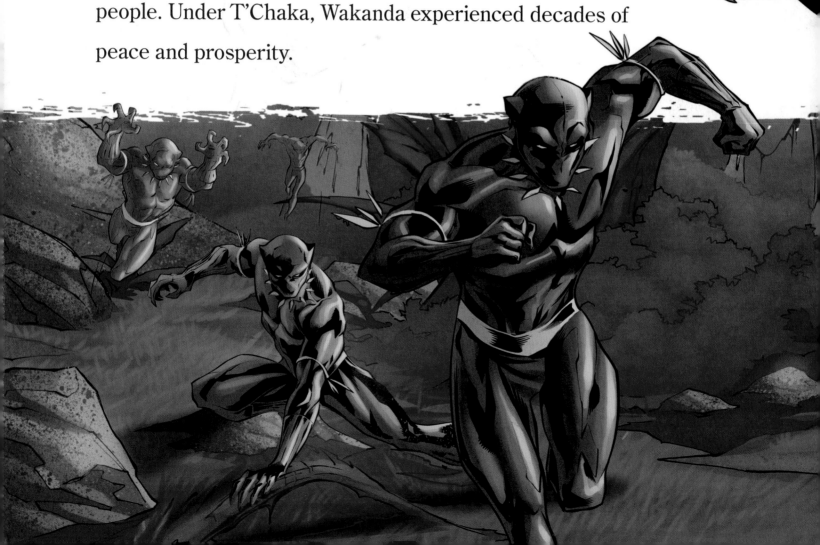

T'Chaka had a son named T'Challa. With his wife, Ramonda, by his side, T'Chaka taught the young prince everything he could. He had very high expectations for his only son.

T'Challa grew up watching his father protect Wakanda. Every day, T'Challa wished he could be just like him— both king *and* protector.

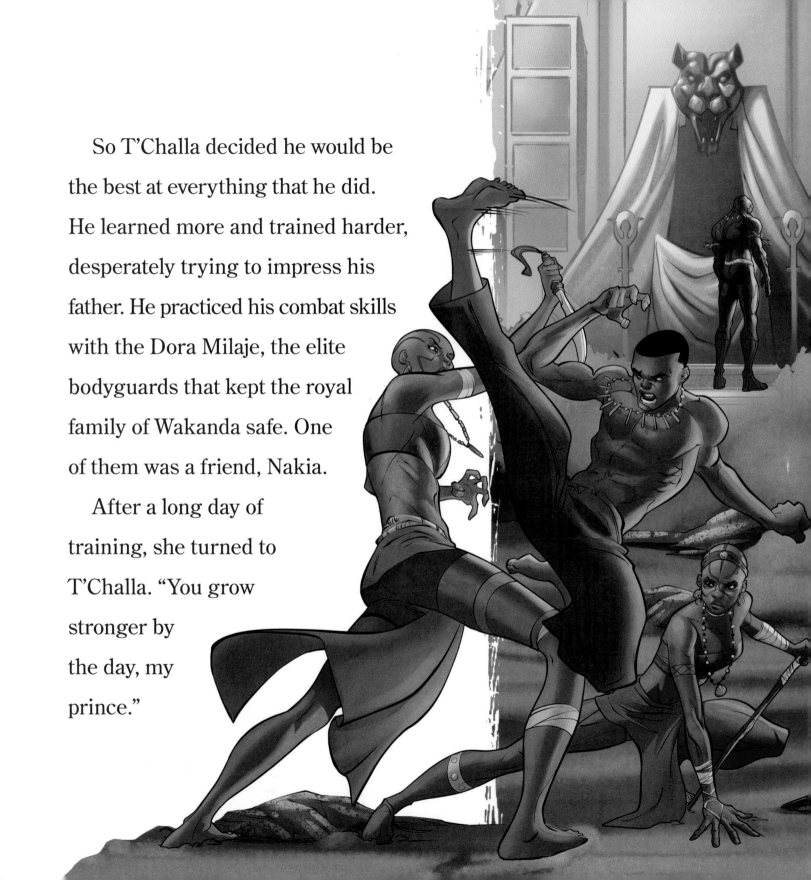

So T'Challa decided he would be the best at everything that he did. He learned more and trained harder, desperately trying to impress his father. He practiced his combat skills with the Dora Milaje, the elite bodyguards that kept the royal family of Wakanda safe. One of them was a friend, Nakia.

After a long day of training, she turned to T'Challa. "You grow stronger by the day, my prince."

Later that day, T'Challa found his father in the palace. He took a deep breath and began to recite the speech he had practiced over and over in his head. "Father, I believe I am ready to take the trials of the Black Panther. The sacred test. I know I can—"

But T'Chaka cut T'Challa off before he could finish. "No. You are not yet ready."

Meanwhile, little did the royal family know, a Super Villain named Klaw was launching an attack on Wakanda. Klaw was a man who had been turned into pure sonic energy, and wore a sonic converter over his right hand. He was constantly invading Wakanda in order to steal their Vibranium. This time, in a well-orchestrated attack, he quickly overpowered the Wakandan military. "Send my regards to the Panther!" he cackled.

"He's getting away!" one of the guards shouted. Klaw had seized the Vibranium and was making his escape. He used his sonic power to carry the Vibranium deep into the Wakandan jungle. His henchmen would be there waiting for him. But T'Chaka was not about to allow Klaw to steal from Wakanda.

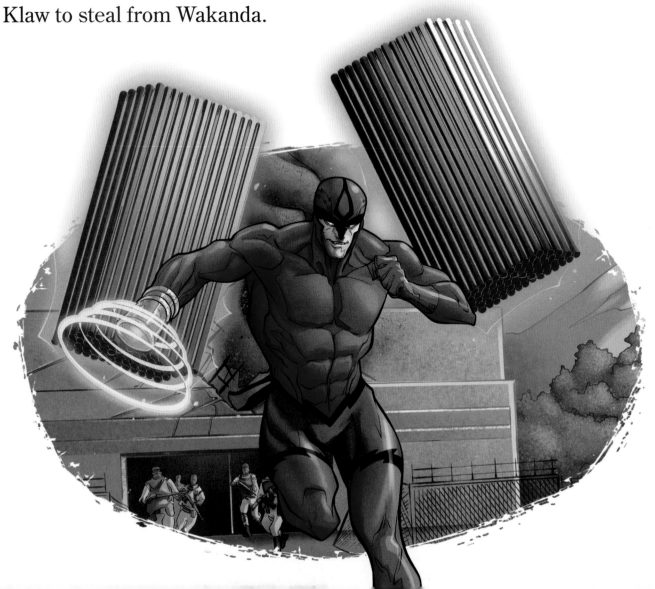

As Black Panther, T'Chaka took to Wakanda's defense. Black Panther's suit allowed him to glide through the jungle undetected. He easily caught up to Klaw and cornered him in a large clearing. "You have stolen from my people," Black Panther boomed. "I promise you shall not have the chance to do so again."

Klaw sneered at his foe. "Ha! You think you have the power to defeat me? Pampered royal. You know nothing."

Black Panther prepared to fight his worst enemy. He knew he had to defeat Klaw once and for all to keep his country safe. Black Panther leaped toward Klaw, but the villain had been expecting the fabled warrior's strike. Klaw aimed his sonic converter and fired, unleashing his full power. *KRAZZK!*

As Black Panther fell back from the sudden blast, he heard a scream. "NOOO!"

It was his son, T'Challa.

T'Challa had followed his father after hearing of Klaw's attack. When he saw that his father was in real danger, he tried to protect him with his Vibranium shield, but it was too late. Black Panther was gravely wounded.

Klaw cackled, his spirits rising at the sight of the fallen king. "What a heartwarming family reunion!" Klaw said as his sonic arm began to whir with power. He aimed it at T'Challa. "Face me, Your Royal Highness!"

KRAZZK! KRAZZK! Klaw began to hit T'Challa with blasts of sonic power as the young prince used his Vibranium shield to absorb them.

"You've made a fatal mistake, Klaw," T'Challa shouted over the deafening booms. "I don't blame you. People do it all the time . . . even my father."

"Oh, really?" Klaw said, smiling. "And what might that mistake be?"

T'Challa narrowed his eyes. "You've underestimated me."

With that, T'Challa raised his shield and brought it down on Klaw's arm, smashing his sonic converter!

"Insolent boy!" Klaw cried. "You'll pay for this."

Klaw took off into the jungle, managing to escape Wakanda once again. T'Challa rushed to his father's side and gently held him in his arms. "Father, please, I need you to know that all my life, I've worked to earn your love and respect. Now I will earn the love and respect of the Wakandan people." T'Challa closed his eyes, whispering one last promise. "Your legacy will live on through me."

And that's exactly what T'Challa did. The young prince became King of Wakanda and passed the Black Panther trials. He donned the Black Panther suit and spent countless years trying to avenge his father.

Those efforts eventually led him to join the Avengers. Although he was now a Super Hero, T'Challa would always be King of Wakanda and the Black Panther.

Mixed Signals from Knowhere

"YOU NEVER HAVE MY BACK!" Star-Lord shouted. The Guardians of the Galaxy were on the *Milano* headed for the space station called Knowhere, when Star-Lord and Drax had gotten into a huge fight—over what, nobody could figure out.

"Why would I?!" Drax shouted back. "You are being ridiculous. Just leave me be. Don't think I won't fight you."

Star-Lord scoffed. "I'm not scared!"

Just then, the emergency distress signal on the communication console started to beep. *Saved by the bell*, Star-Lord thought.

Rocket was already sourcing the signal over at the console. "It's coming from right here . . . on Knowhere," he said to the Guardians.

Drax frowned. "Well, is it somewhere or nowhere?"

Star-Lord's temper flared again. "It's somewhere on Knowhere."

When they stepped off the ship, Star-Lord turned to Drax. "We will finish this later. Right now we have a job to do."

The Guardians followed the signal to a mangled building with a giant hole in its side. Just then, *BOOM!*—a blast knocked the Guardians off their feet. Star-Lord looked up to see Iron Man.

"Can you tell Tony to knock it off?" Star-Lord asked.

"Of course I can," Thor replied, swinging his hammer defensively as Iron Man shot a blast his way.

"Well, what are you waiting for?" Rocket yelled.

"You'll see," Thor said, "in three . . . two . . . ONE!"

At that moment, a green blur jumped out from a building behind Iron Man and slammed into the rampaging Avenger, knocking him to the ground.

"Hulk SMASH!"

It was the mighty Thor!

"Wow, maybe Star-Lord's telepathic?" Rocket said, looking up at Thor.

"Or maybe I was on a mission on Xandar and heard the same distress signal you did," Thor replied.

"Speaking of which," Gamora said, "a little help, please?"

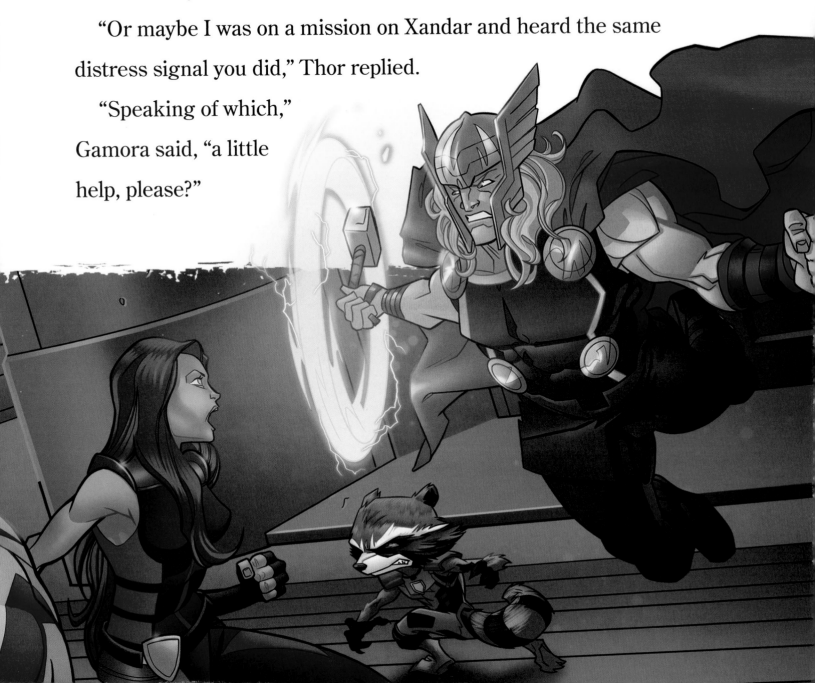

Groot was confused. "I am Groot?"

"You're right, Iron Man is our friend," Rocket replied, "but we can't let him destroy the entire space station!"

"Something's wrong," Gamora said. "Iron Man is a hero."

"Yeah well, somebody should tell him that!" Star-Lord yelled, as he shot another blast at Iron Man.

The Guardians continued to take turns dodging Iron Man's attacks. Then, suddenly, a voice boomed overhead. "Need a hand?"

"Oh, good," Star-Lord said.
"Reinforcements!"

"I don't think he's here to help," Gamora
said, as Iron Man turned and fired a huge
blast at the building. "He's attacking!"

Hulk roared as he squished his friend Iron Man into the ground with his enormous fist.

"I believe you've met Hulk?" Thor said to the Guardians. He motioned to the green giant holding down Iron Man.

"I am Groot," Groot whispered to Rocket.

"You're one to talk," Rocket replied. "You're pretty weird-looking too."

"Only one way to find out," Star-Lord said, bending down to open Iron Man's helmet. There was no one inside. The suit was empty!

"That's what I was trying to tell Thor." Tony Stark's voice came through Thor's communicator. "This is the spare drone I keep on the *Milano* for deep-space missions. JARVIS just told me that it's malfunctioning."

"Malfunctioning," Star-Lord snorted. "You could say that."

"What a relief! Now, let's get this suit back to Tony," Thor said.

"Great, bye!" Gamora replied. "Now, we have some Guardians stuff to take care of." She turned to Star-Lord. "Drax thinks you mean he literally needs to have your back."

Drax frowned. "Your back is small and weak."

Star-Lord hung his head. "Uh, it's a figure of speech. I'm sorry, man. I guess we were all a little mixed up today."

ULTRON GOES VIRAL

ALARM BELLS RANG throughout Avengers Tower.

Earth was in a state of emergency.

Something horrific and unspeakable had happened. Something

nobody should ever experience in their lifetime.

"The Internet is down!" Iron Man shouted over the roar of the

alarms. He had gathered the heroes on the roof of Avengers Tower.

Thor was confused. "So, humans can't watch their kitten videos?"

"All vital Earth systems need Internet," Black Widow said grimly. "Hospitals, the electrical grid, you name it."

Captain America stepped forward, taking charge. "Hulk and Black Widow, check in with the police. Falcon, maintain the hospitals. Thor and Hawkeye, keep an eye out for trouble. Iron Man, you're with me. Let's go!"

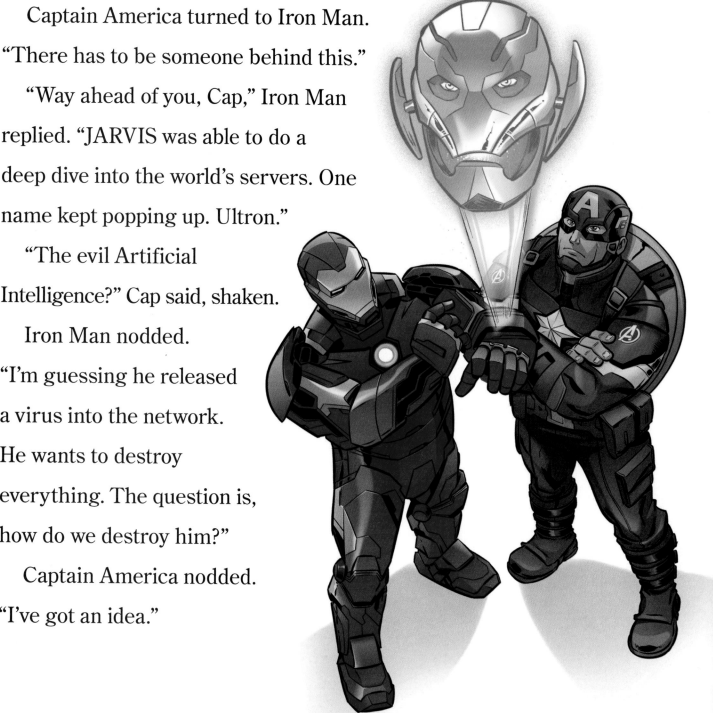

Captain America turned to Iron Man. "There has to be someone behind this."

"Way ahead of you, Cap," Iron Man replied. "JARVIS was able to do a deep dive into the world's servers. One name kept popping up. Ultron."

"The evil Artificial Intelligence?" Cap said, shaken.

Iron Man nodded. "I'm guessing he released a virus into the network. He wants to destroy everything. The question is, how do we destroy him?"

Captain America nodded. "I've got an idea."

With Iron Man using his rocket boots and Cap on his sky-cycle, they headed toward their destination.

"I know you're a genius, Tony," Cap said, "but we need smarts *and* power. We need Captain Marvel."

"I've heard of her," Iron Man asked. "What's her deal?"

"She's the head of Alpha Flight," Captain America replied. "She's an astronaut, half-alien, and won't back down for anyone. Oh, and she lives in the Statue of Liberty's crown."

When they arrived at the Statue of Liberty, they found Captain Marvel straightening her uniform. "Internet's down across the globe, and it's a complete mess," she said, not bothering to say hello first. "I assume that's why you boys are here?"

"Ultron released a virus," Iron Man explained, also not wasting words.

Captain Marvel nodded. She understood immediately. "I'm on it. Meet me at Alpha Flight Headquarters."

She grabbed her official Alpha Flight communicator. "Alpha Flight, prepare for my arrival." Captain Marvel then launched herself into the sky without even noticing Cap and Iron Man trying to catch up.

"How can her communicator be working?" Captain America asked as he and Iron Man tailed Captain Marvel.

"Alpha Flight must have bypassed the traditional network system, similar to JARVIS. I'm not surprised. Alpha Flight has some of the best tech around," Iron Man said. "Well, after Stark Industries, of course."

Cap smiled. "Of course."

Captain Marvel looked over her shoulder. "Come on, keep up!" The three heroes soared through the air and arrived at Alpha Flight Headquarters.

Alpha Flight gleamed with cutting-edge technology. Scientists, astronauts, engineers, and soldiers hurried to and fro.

Captain America and Iron Man watched in admiration as Captain Marvel strode into the room and immediately began issuing orders.

"Gonzalez!" she said. "Get an encrypted pipeline. O'Connell! Initiate offensive network protocol 616."

Iron Man watched code scroll along the monitors. "It's digital warfare," he explained to Cap. "She's hunting Ultron's virus."

Soon everyone could see the plan was working. "Yes!" Captain Marvel yelled at her screen.

"Ultron is going to see where the threat is coming from," Iron Man warned her. "He'll come here to physically shut us down."

Captain Marvel smiled. "Let him come."

BOOM! Suddenly the wall behind Captain America exploded. Ultron appeared through the dust and mayhem. "Oh, how cute," he said. "Iron Man and Captain America think they can foil my genius plot to destroy human civilization."

Ultron grabbed Cap's shield, catching him off guard. But the hero wasn't about to give up so easily. "Bad idea, buddy."

Ultron just laughed as Captain America leaped into action. He flung his shield at Ultron and hit him with a powerful punch. But Ultron was too strong. He grabbed Captain America and threw him out of the building through the massive hole in the wall!

Cap dangled off the side of the building as Ultron turned to Iron Man and the Alpha Flight team. "Give up, puny humans. Your Earth systems don't stand a chance. Nobody can protect humanity now!"

It was a fearsome speech, but suddenly Iron Man began to laugh. "You've never met Captain Marvel, have you?"

Ultron sneered, looking at Captain Marvel. "This human woman and her pathetic little friends? I will destroy them!"

Captain Marvel glared at Ultron. Then, tightening her gloves, she nodded at her first lieutenant.

"I'm only half-human," Captain Marvel said as the lieutenant hit the button that said EXECUTE.

Ultron squinted his robotic eyes. "I'm not impress— Oof!" He grunted in surprise as Captain Marvel punched him right in the face.

She grinned. "Come on, you hunk of junk, let's— GAH!"

Ultron tackled her to the ground with a *CRASH!* Their fight raged all over Alpha Flight Headquarters as everyone scrambled for cover. Before long, both were bruised and battered. One of Captain Marvel's strongest punches had put a big dent in Ultron's cheek!

"This is getting boring," Captain Marvel said. "And since my code is nearly done executing . . ."

BING! the computer announced.

"There we go," Captain Marvel said, smiling sweetly. "Your virus is toast, Ultron. And so are you."

Captain Marvel swung a mighty punch. The blow was so powerful that Ultron burst through the wall and sailed straight into space!

"What'd I miss?" Captain America asked as he made his way back up to Headquarters. Captain Marvel and Iron Man looked at each other and burst out laughing. Tony had to take off his helmet in order to catch his breath.

"Up high," Tony said, raising a hand.

"The Internet's back up," she said, high-fiving Tony, "and Ultron is out of our hair. Great work today, heroes!"

Tony smiled. "Sorry, Steve, but it looks like the Avengers have a new Captain now."

The Incredible Spider-Hulk

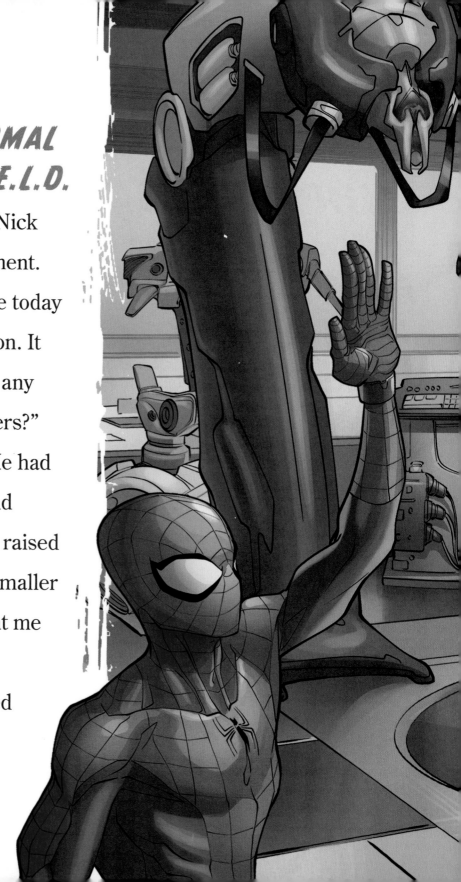

IT WAS A NORMAL DAY AT S.H.I.E.L.D.

Headquarters when Nick Fury made a big announcement. "Heroes, I've called you here today to unveil our newest invention. It can swap your abilities with any hero. Do I have any volunteers?"

Hulk couldn't believe it. He had been feeling a bit bulky—and angry!—lately. But when he raised his hand, he also noticed a smaller red one shoot up, too. "Count me in, Nicky!"

"Spider boy!" Thor shouted gleefully.

Project A.S.S.E.M.B.L.E.
Ability Switching and
Super-Power Exchange
Mighty Big Laser Engine.

"Come on, dude. It's Spider-MAN!" Spider-Man said.

Nick Fury smiled. "Welcome, Spider-Man. Thank you for volunteering. Please stand next to Hulk on the big red *X*."

Hulk and Spider-Man walked over to where they were told.

"Stand still," Fury commanded. "This might hurt a little."

Hulk and Spider-Man looked at each other, eyes wide with fear, as Fury activated the device.

Suddenly the machine began to overheat, causing a massive explosion that shook the room! When the smoke cleared, a strange figure emerged. It wasn't Spider-Man. It wasn't Hulk. It looked like both of them . . . combined. Two heroes had merged into one hybrid creature—the Spider-Hulk!

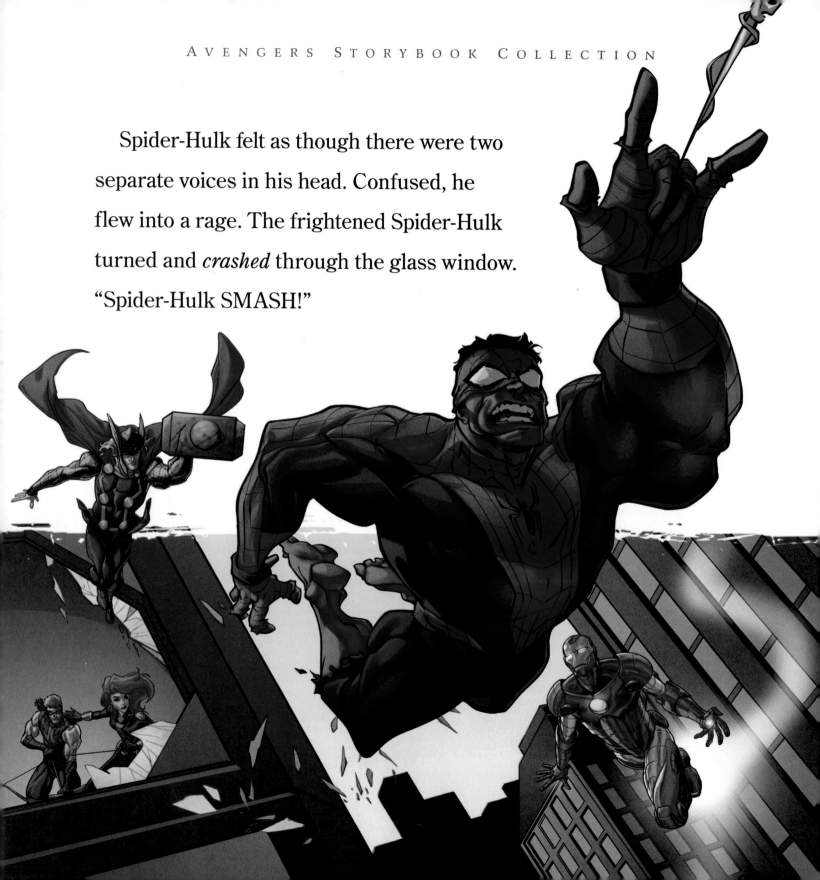

Spider-Hulk felt as though there were two separate voices in his head. Confused, he flew into a rage. The frightened Spider-Hulk turned and *crashed* through the glass window. "Spider-Hulk SMASH!"

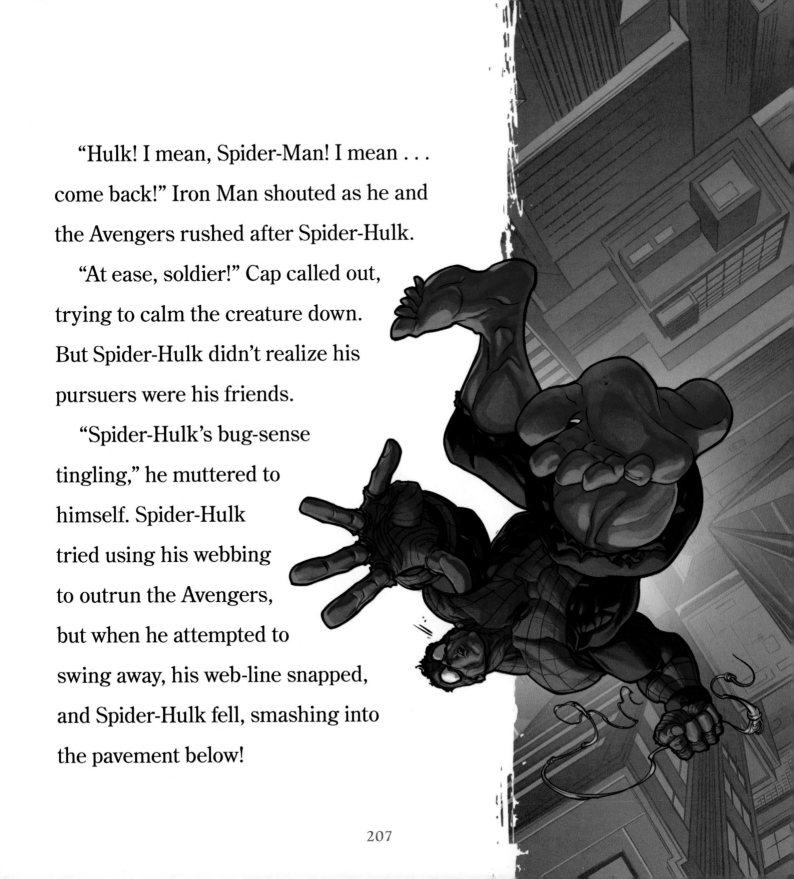

"Hulk! I mean, Spider-Man! I mean . . . come back!" Iron Man shouted as he and the Avengers rushed after Spider-Hulk.

"At ease, soldier!" Cap called out, trying to calm the creature down. But Spider-Hulk didn't realize his pursuers were his friends.

"Spider-Hulk's bug-sense tingling," he muttered to himself. Spider-Hulk tried using his webbing to outrun the Avengers, but when he attempted to swing away, his web-line snapped, and Spider-Hulk fell, smashing into the pavement below!

With Spider-Hulk momentarily weakened, Hawkeye quickly came up with a plan. Sometimes when Hulk got too angry, he would calm him down with a story. So Hawkeye sat down and pulled out a book to read to Spider-Hulk. It worked too well. The hybrid hero thought it was bedtime, and he fled looking for a midnight snack!

When Thor and Black Widow finally caught up with Spider-Hulk, he was ransacking every hot dog cart in the city looking for snacks.

"Mmmm . . . Spider-Hulk loves hot dogs," Spider-Hulk said as he shoved six hot dogs into his mouth.

That gave Black Widow an idea. "We can lure Spider-Hulk back," she whispered to Thor. "We'll use the one thing both Spider-Man and the Hulk love. *Food*."

"Got the chocolate cake!" Thor announced.

"Shhh!" Black Widow whispered. "We need to use the cake to lure him back without scaring him away. It'll be a piece of cake. . . . Get it?"

Thor squinted in concentration. "Uh, I think so."

Spider-Hulk turned his head toward the noise. Black Widow and Thor froze as he cautiously approached the duo.

The heroes had successfully lured Spider-Hulk into their trap.
But before Thor could lead the way back to headquarters,
Spider-Hulk swallowed the entire cake whole!

Talk about a cake-tastrophy, Iron Man laughed to himself. *Wait, I've got it! Wheat cakes!* Iron Man knew that Spider-Man was really Peter Parker, a teenager who couldn't resist his Aunt May's famous wheat cakes. He flew to the Avengers Tower kitchen and asked his chef to set about making enough wheat cakes to feed a small country. In other words, enough wheat cakes to feed one Spider-Hulk.

Then, with his wheat cakes in tow, Iron Man zoomed around the city. He left a trail of wheat cakes for Spider-Hulk to follow all the way back to S.H.I.E.L.D. headquarters. Captain America followed closely behind Spider-Hulk. He quietly radioed the other Avengers, "It's working. We're on our way back."

Finally, Spider-Hulk was safely back in S.H.I.E.L.D. Headquarters. The team advanced toward him, but Captain America held them off.

"Stay back," Cap said. "I wouldn't want anyone to get caught in the cross fire of his monstrous appetite."

Slowly, little by little, Spider-Hulk made his way toward the lab as the Avengers tiptoed behind him.

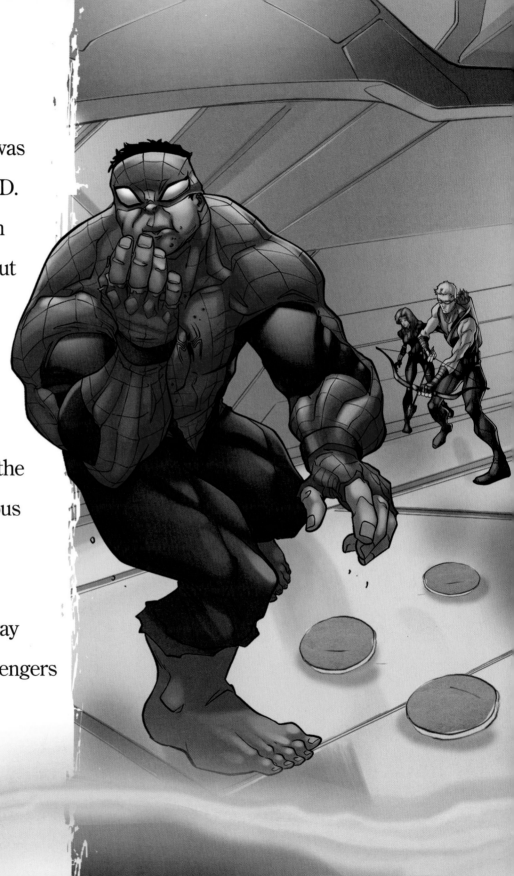

Spider-Hulk continued to chomp down as he followed the trail of wheat cakes.

"Almost there," Iron Man said to Nick Fury when they got to the lab. "Just a few more. . . ."

Then Spider-Hulk reached the center of the lab and plopped down to enjoy the rest of his snack. Spider-Hulk was so distracted that he didn't notice he was sitting on the big red *X*. He swallowed the wheat cake and said, "Spider-Hulk wants maple—" But before he could finish, Nick Fury pressed REVERSE.

With a loud crack and a sizzle of electricity, Spider-Hulk began to separate. When the light faded, two heroes stepped forth: Spider-Man and the Hulk.

The Avengers cheered for their two—very different—friends. Everything was finally back to normal.

Hulk put his massive arm around Spider-Man's shoulder. "Glad to be Hulk again," he said.

"Yeah, I think I like being me," Spider-Man replied.

Hulk grinned from ear to ear. "But Bug-Man's appetite is as puny as Bug-Man. Hulk hungry!"

THE GIRL WHO WAS HEADED to Avengers Tower with a platter of cookies didn't look like anything special.

Well, that's not quite true. She looked like a squirrel. She had a big, bushy tail and buck teeth. But the point is, she didn't look like an especially powerful squirrel. Even though she was.

The young woman marching toward Avengers Tower was in fact the Unbeatable Squirrel Girl!

When the girl reached Avengers Tower, she found the heroes standing outside. She couldn't believe it!

"A Girl Scout!" Thor said, noticing her.

"It's Squirrel Girl, actually," she responded. "And I'm here to join the Avengers. I made cookies. See?"

"Doreen Green," Iron Man said, recognizing her. "Thor, this is no Girl Scout. Doreen has the powers of a squirrel."

Squirrel Girl nodded eagerly as Thor took a cookie. "Yep! And I—"

BRRRRING! Suddenly Bruce Banner's gadget went off.

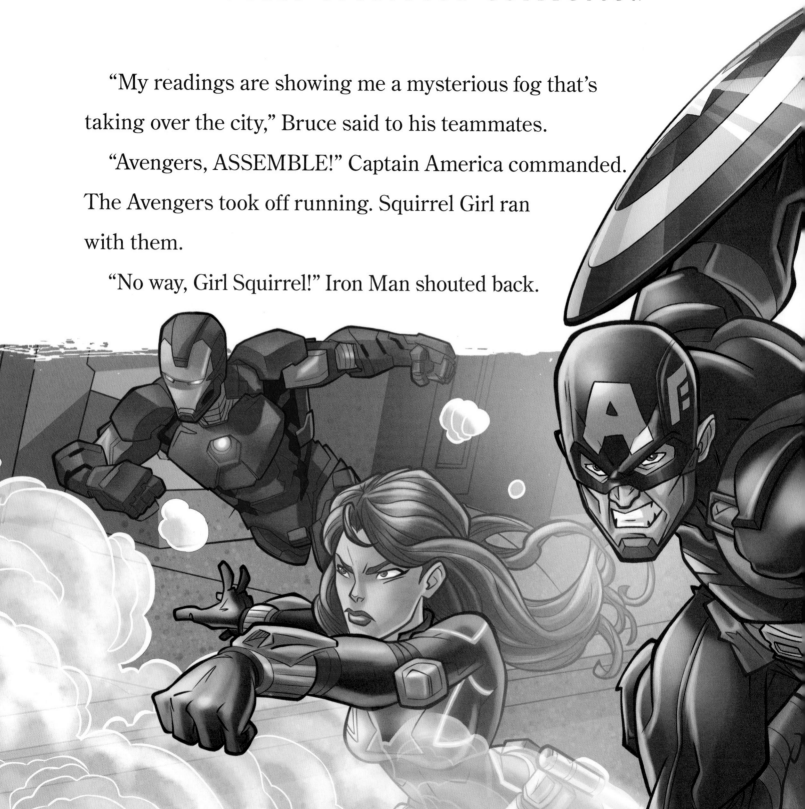

"My readings are showing me a mysterious fog that's taking over the city," Bruce said to his teammates.

"Avengers, ASSEMBLE!" Captain America commanded. The Avengers took off running. Squirrel Girl ran with them.

"No way, Girl Squirrel!" Iron Man shouted back.

"It's Squirrel Girl!" she corrected. "And I want to help!"

As the Avengers ran ahead, Bruce Banner pulled Squirrel Girl aside. "Look, I'm sorry, Doreen, but you aren't battle-tested," he said.

"But!" Squirrel Girl said.

Banner shook his head. "Go home." Then, with a huge roar, he transformed into the Hulk and ran off to join the other heroes.

Squirrel Girl was all alone.
"But I know I can do it," she
said. Why wouldn't the Avengers
take a chance on her? Her
shoulders slumped. Her
heart sank.

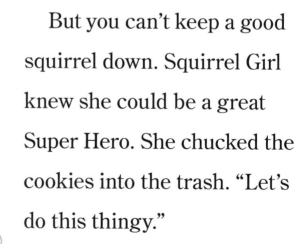

But you can't keep a good
squirrel down. Squirrel Girl
knew she could be a great
Super Hero. She chucked the
cookies into the trash. "Let's
do this thingy."

It wasn't long until Doreen reached the thick, white fog. It was so dense, she could barely see.

"Something isn't right here," Squirrel Girl said. "This fog seems . . . unnatural. What's causing it? I need to get a better look."

With the agility of a super-powered squirrel, she launched herself onto the side of a skyscraper. Squirrel Girl continued to climb up, up, up until she was above the thick white clouds.

Meanwhile, the city was in chaos. But in the middle of the fog the Avengers were busy saving the day. Iron Man and Falcon swooped through the air while shouting orders down below.

Captain America and Black Widow protected civilians. Hulk picked up cars and placed them in parking spots like they were toys. All while Thor stood at the center of the street trying to stop the fog with his mighty hammer. Lightning and thunder erupted from his hammer into the sky. But the harder he tried, the thicker the fog became.

Using her enhanced squirrel-vision, Squirrel Girl gazed out over the streets of Manhattan.

"Now, if I was an evil weatherman, where would I be . . . ?"

Bingo! The fog had cleared enough for Squirrel Girl to see masked men running into a store.

"Gross. Who wears green to a robbery and— OMG! It's Hydra."

Squirrel Girl had read about these guys. They tried to destroy the city with a destruction ray. They were super evil.

"This is big. Huge!" Squirrel Girl said quietly to herself. "I'm going to need some help."

Squirrel Girl jumped off the roof of the skyscraper and began to leap from building to building. She moved through the New York City skyline like a squirrel in the treetops. As she went, she emitted her chittering squirrel call. Every squirrel in Manhattan heard it and came running.

By the time Squirrel Girl reached the building that Hydra was robbing, a huge swarm of squirrels was following her. Sometimes it was good to be a squirrel.

"A jewelry store!" Squirrel Girl said to her squirrel friends. Then Squirrel Girl straightened and flashed a giant grin.

"Squirrels . . . ASSEMBLE!"

The squirrels looked around, confused. Squirrel Girl scrunched her face. "Sorry. That sounded a lot cooler in my head."

"Halt!" Squirrel Girl yelled as she marched into the jewelry store. The Hydra goons, who were carrying heavy sacks out of the store, froze.

"That's . . . a lot of squirrels," one of them said.

"You better believe it," Squirrel Girl said. "Sic 'em, guys!" Squirrel Girl and her army of squirrels attacked.

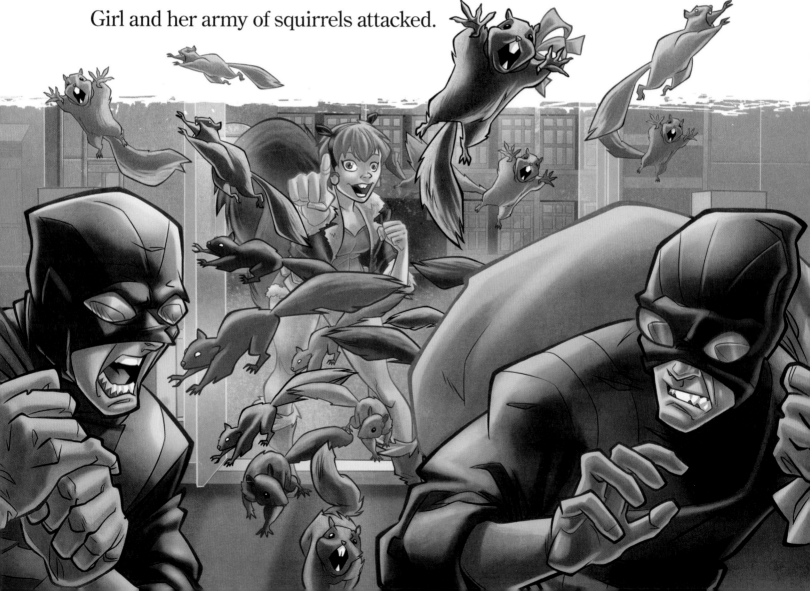

Soon the fight was over. Squirrel Girl was tying the villains all up when she found a weird gadget. "A weather machine?" Squirrel Girl said, crushing it under her foot.

"I knew it! *You* guys created the fog. But what were you stealing . . . ?" she said, making her way into the store.

"Wow." Her voice dropped to a whisper. "Tippy-Toe, go get the Avengers."

A while later, the Avengers came running into the store.

"The fog is gone for now," Captain America said to his teammates. "But where is Squirrel Girl?"

"In here, guys!" Squirrel Girl called out cheerfully. She was splashing around in an enormous pile of sparkly diamonds!

Iron Man snapped his metal fingers. "The fog was a diversion. Hydra needed these diamonds for their new destruction ray."

"They would have succeeded too," Cap said, "if it wasn't for Squirrel Girl."

Klaw's Revenge

WHOOSH! Black Panther leaped out of the Quinjet, swiftly catching himself on a branch.

Exhaling a sigh of relief, he quickly moved through the lush jungles of Wakanda, his African home. He was returning after a long time away fighting crime with the Avengers. As much as he enjoyed working with a team, T'Challa was happiest when he was in Wakanda.

T'Challa was still settling into his role as king and Black Panther. He had vowed to honor his father's legacy, but trying to live up to his greatness was taking a toll. T'Challa's father was able to be both king and protector, making him beloved by his people. It was a difficult job, but T'Challa was determined to serve his country like his father before him.

After sorting out another crisis with the Avengers, I can only presume I'll find more here at home, T'Challa thought. *A Black Panther's work is never done.*

When T'Challa arrived home, he found his stepmother, Ramonda, waiting for him. "Welcome home, my son," she said, wrapping him in a big hug. But T'Challa was tense. Ramonda could tell something was on his mind. Before she could pry further, two figures *burst* through the door. It was Okoye and Nakia, two of the Dora Milaje, warrior women sworn to protect the Wakandan king.

"Sire, there's an emergency!" Okoye shouted.

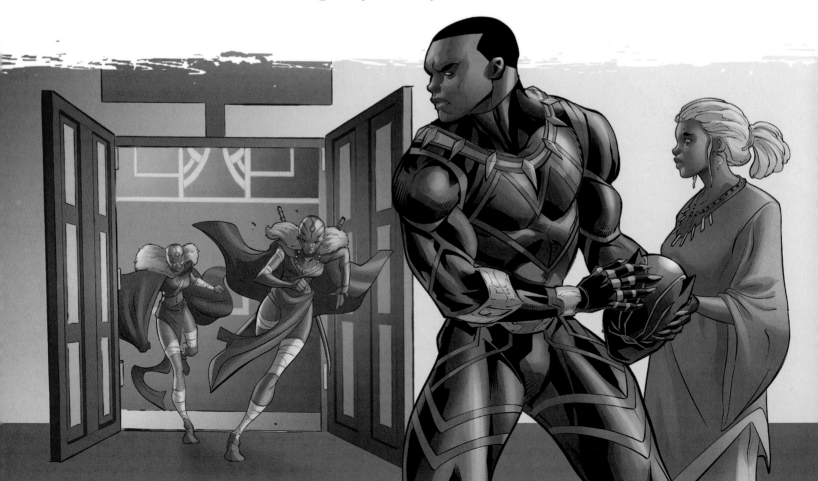

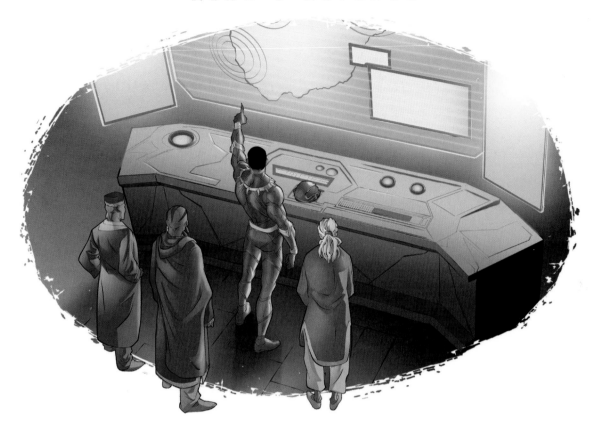

T'Challa and Ramonda quickly followed the Dora Milaje to the council room. There they found the tribal elders gathered around a large monitor. Everyone spoke in hushed tones as T'Challa approached the monitor.

"These energy readings are off the charts," T'Challa said as he assessed the situation. "The spikes look almost as if they're following a path and it's headed straight for us."

"There's only one person who could be behind this," T'Challa said. *"Klaw."*

Everyone in the council chamber gasped. Klaw was Wakanda's greatest enemy and the only outsider ever to infiltrate its walls. The last time Klaw was in Wakanda, he had defeated T'Challa's father. T'Challa chased away the painful memory.

"Okoye. Nakia. Come with me. We need to stop Klaw before he reaches the palace," T'Challa said, pulling on his mask. "Let's go!"

Meanwhile, Klaw was blasting his way underground using his sonic-powered arm. It was only a matter of time before he made it to the palace. And Klaw had only one thing on his mind. *Revenge.*

Little did Klaw know, Black Panther had been preparing for his next attack. Black Panther gave Nakia and Okoye specific instructions. They were to go to his lab, grab the metal sphere on his desk, and be ready for his signal.

Then Black Panther led giant trucks loaded with long Vibranium rods out of the city. "This way, toward the energy spikes!" Black Panther commanded. They would cut Klaw off on his way into Wakanda.

Black Panther saw the ground in the distance being ripped apart by glowing sonic energy.

"Quickly! Get into your positions," Black Panther shouted over the deafening roar of Klaw's charge. The Vibranium's sound-absorbing properties had the power to destroy Klaw's sonic form. It was the only thing that *could* stop him.

"NOW!" Black Panther shouted. With that, the trucks plunged the Vibranium rods straight into the ground. *BOOM!* Klaw ran into the Vibranium rods underground and jolted back violently. As he flew up from the dirt, Klaw cried out in pain. "Nooooooooo!"

Black Panther leaped off the truck and approached the motionless Klaw. As Black Panther kneeled down, Klaw sprang to his feet, knocking Black Panther off-balance. The hero quickly recovered, landing in a warrior stance. The two enemies squared off: Black Panther versus Klaw—the ultimate showdown.

"Hello, old friend," Klaw taunted. "As fate would have it, I was actually headed to the palace to see you. But I guess this place is as good as any to finally destroy the heir to the Wakandan throne."

"Funny," Black Panther replied. "I don't plan on giving up my throne anytime soon."

BOOMPH! With a mighty kick, Black Panther sent Klaw flying through the air. Black Panther was extremely skilled in the art of combat. Klaw didn't stand a chance.

Well, at least that's what Black Panther thought. Though Klaw did not match his foe in brute strength, he made up for it with his powerful sonic arm. It could send dangerous blasts of pure sound that would stun his enemies.

"Is that all you got, Black Panther?" Klaw sneered. He drew back his arm as it began to whir with power. In the blink of an eye, the villain launched a thunderous blast toward Black Panther. The hero slammed into the ground.

"Ha-ha-ha!" Klaw's laughter echoed through the valley. He approached Black Panther, who had fallen onto his back. Black Panther groaned in pain. "Silly child. When you destroyed my arm all those years ago, I vowed to take my revenge on the nation of Wakanda. And your end shall be my final act."

Like a flash of lightning, Black Panther's legs smashed into the villain. The king had given Klaw a taste of his own medicine. "That's your problem, Klaw," Black Panther growled. "You talk too much."

Black Panther watched as Klaw's body soared through the air. It was exactly what Black Panther had planned. "Nakia. Okoye. The sphere!"

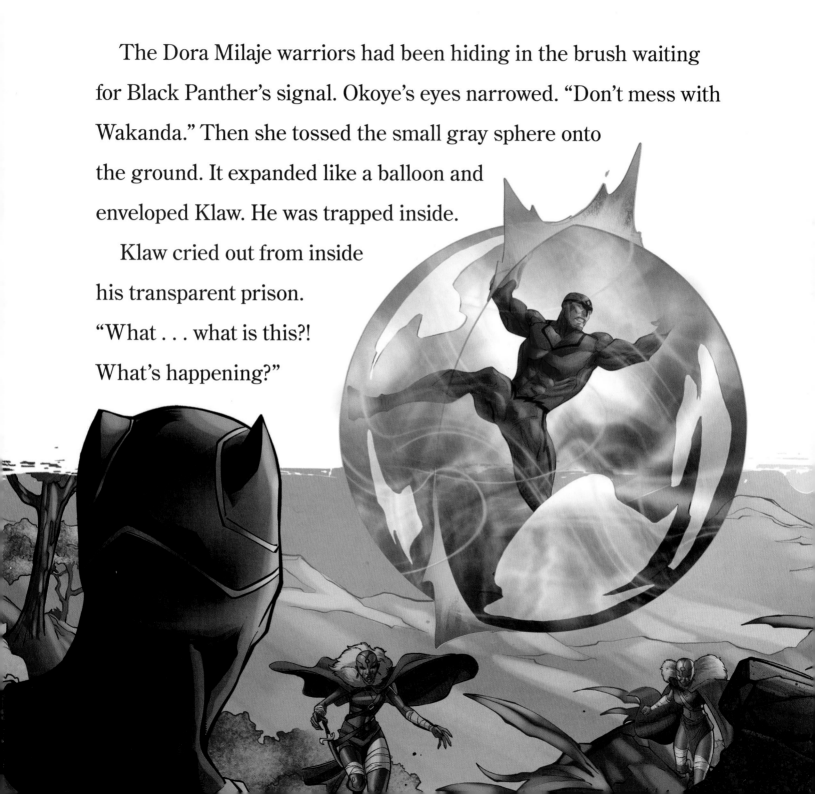

The Dora Milaje warriors had been hiding in the brush waiting for Black Panther's signal. Okoye's eyes narrowed. "Don't mess with Wakanda." Then she tossed the small gray sphere onto the ground. It expanded like a balloon and enveloped Klaw. He was trapped inside.

Klaw cried out from inside his transparent prison. "What . . . what is this?! What's happening?"

Black Panther placed his hands on his hips proudly. "It's my latest invention. A spherical prison made entirely of Vibranium. I knew you'd be back, Klaw. I came prepared."

With Klaw locked away for good, Black Panther gathered his people in the city square. They cheered as their king rose to speak. "Our nation has faced many threats over the years. Although I cannot promise the threats will end, I do promise to protect you like my father before me. I promise to continue his legacy by working to live up to his greatness—not only as a king, but as *Black Panther*."

From Here to Infinity

THE AVENGERS were feeling a bit uneasy. They had each been called to assemble on the S.H.I.E.L.D. Helicarrier by Nick Fury. The message from the director was vague, but the heroes understood why the organization was so secretive. Everything at S.H.I.E.L.D. was classified information.

So while the Avengers were used to surprise missions, this one felt different.

Nick Fury's tone was grim. "There's no easy way to say this, but the universe is in danger."

Iron Man frowned. "What else is new?"

"Thanos," Fury replied. The villain's hologram instantly shimmered into view.

"Thanos is looking for the Infinity Stones," Nick Fury continued. "Each stone is unique. Power, space, time, mind, soul, and reality. He has four of them. He still needs reality and space. I'm told he's on Astra, searching. If he finds them, Thanos will place them in his gauntlet. The fate of the universe will literally be in his hands."

There was a long silence. Then Captain America cleared his throat to speak. "Avengers, ASSEMBLE!"

"Aren't we *Earth's* Mightiest Heroes?" Hawkeye asked as they rocketed away. "Space isn't really our thing."

"We shall have the element of surpise!" Thor noted cheerfully.

However, when they landed, Thanos was waiting for them.

"Ah, just in time!" he bellowed, his gauntlet lifting him into the air.

"Surprise!" Hawkeye shouted, shooting an arrow at the villain.

But it simply bounced off.

The Avengers watched with horror as Thanos's gauntlet began to glow even brighter. As if in slow motion, Thanos shot a powerful energy beam directly at Iron Man! The hero crashed to the ground.

"Let me at him!" Captain America said, throwing his shield at Thanos. But, again, it had no effect.

One by one, the rest of the Avengers continued to attack. First, Black Widow fired her Widow's Sting at Thanos, who simply brushed it off like it was static electricity. Then Thor called lightning down from the sky, but the villain raised his gauntlet and absorbed it without flinching.

Rising weakly, Iron Man looked up at Thanos. "He's . . . unstoppable."

"My turn," Hulk snarled, unfazed. "Hulk SMASH!"

Hulk's fists slammed down onto the planet's hard surface. The ground rattled and cracked, buckling under Thanos, but he didn't falter. Instead, he targeted a fiery burst of energy at Hulk. The giant hero stumbled backward. Then the evil Thanos used his powerful fist to punch Hulk right in the face!!

Hulk was bruised. Iron Man's thrusters were fried. Cap's shield was battered. Thor's arm ached. Black Widow's wrists hurt. And Hawkeye had only one arrow.

"Nothing's working," Black Widow said, breathing heavily.

Thor's shoulders slumped. "The villain has only four stones! Imagine if he had all six."

Cap looked at his defeated friends. He had never felt like this before. He felt . . . hopeless.

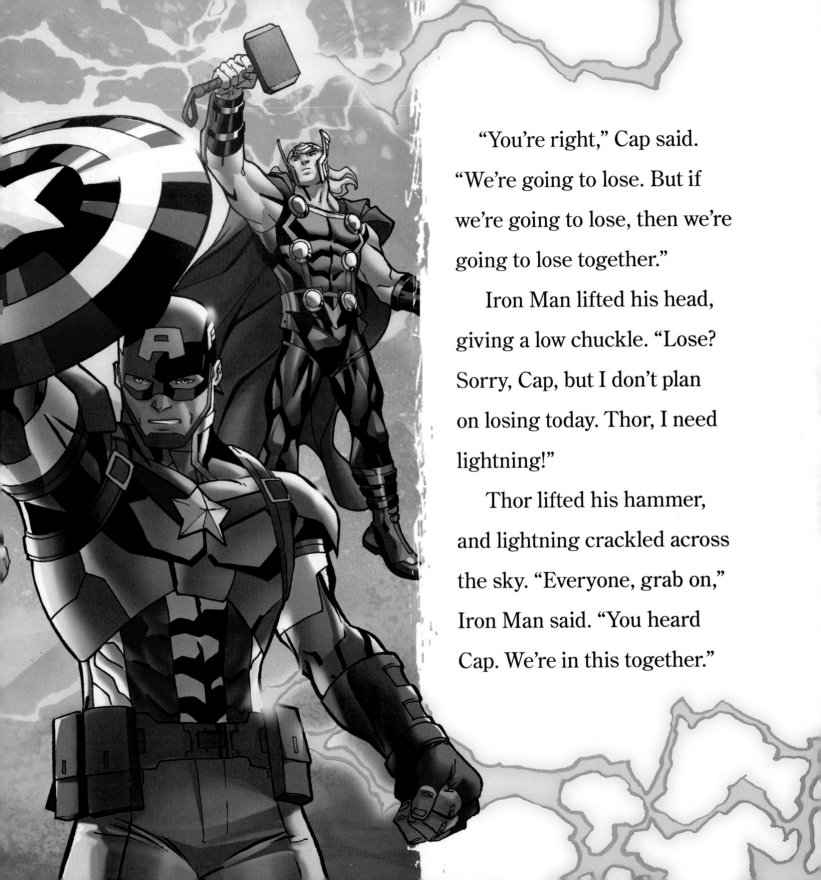

"You're right," Cap said. "We're going to lose. But if we're going to lose, then we're going to lose together."

Iron Man lifted his head, giving a low chuckle. "Lose? Sorry, Cap, but I don't plan on losing today. Thor, I need lightning!"

Thor lifted his hammer, and lightning crackled across the sky. "Everyone, grab on," Iron Man said. "You heard Cap. We're in this together."

Content that the pesky Avengers were out of the way, Thanos admired his Infinity Stones. "I'm so close," he whispered to himself. "Just two more, and I will have infinite power."

SHOOM! Thanos blinked at the sound of metal cutting through the air. He saw Captain America holding his shield. It glowed and vibrated with pure, golden power.

"This shield holds the combined power of the Avengers. Cool, huh?" Cap said.

Thanos smiled, then sent a blast from his wrist. But it bounced off the shield, throwing Thanos into the air.

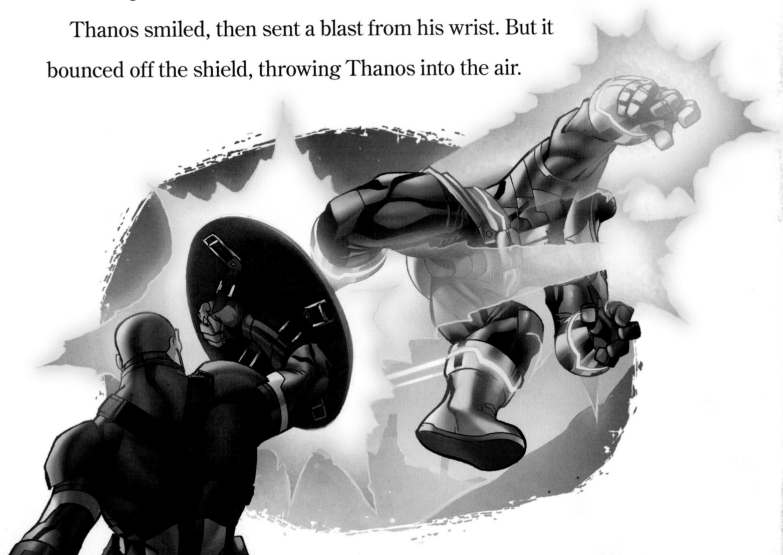

The Avengers had to act quickly while Thanos was down. Turning to Hulk, Iron Man said, "Okay, big guy, you're up!"

Hulk took Captain America's shield, still infused with the Avengers' powers, and hurled it mightily at Thanos, aiming for the Infinity Gauntlet on his raised fist.

Thanos saw the oncoming shield and quickly tried to deflect the blow. But the shield, now powered by multiple sources and propelled by Hulk's super strength, struck Thanos's hand with a fiery explosion that knocked the gauntlet right off. It fell to the ground, dislodging the four Infinity Stones. Black Widow quickly grabbed the fallen Stones. When Thanos realized he was defeated, he grabbed his gauntlet and vanished.

"Where is big purple man?" Hulk asked back on the ship.

"It's not over," Cap said. "Thanos will be back. But we'll be ready. For now, let's get these Stones to S.H.I.E.L.D."

"I'm not worried," Iron Man said. "Six rainbow rocks versus six powerful heroes?"

Hawkeye laughed. "You mean six of *Earth's* Mightiest Heroes!"

A MARVELOUS DUO

"**AGHHHH!" KAMALA KHAN SCREAMED** as she slammed her fist against the school building. She had just failed a major Biology test. "That Super Villain kept me up all night. I should've studied," she muttered to herself. Only a few people knew, but Kamala was secretly the Super Hero Ms. Marvel! She had the power to stretch, morph, and heal. Her fists were powerful. Just ask the wall.

"Ms. Marvel," a deep voice suddenly boomed. Kamala turned to see a strange man wearing a coat and hat. "Come with me."

Kamala was shocked. How did he know her Super Hero name? He must have been looking for trouble. Her temper flared again. "All right, let's go, big guy!"

"Excellent," the man said, cheerfully. "I shall lead the— WHOA!" He yelled in surprise as Kamala threw a punch right at his face.

As the man ducked the blow, his tattered hat and coat fell away. Kamala gasped. Standing in front of her was the mighty Thor!

"Kamala, I apologize for approaching you in disguise. I was trying to 'keep a low profile,' as Hawkeye puts it," Thor said. "But I have urgent news. A Super Villain named the Inventor is here in Jersey City. He has been kidnapping teenagers and turning them into—"

"I'm gonna stop you right there," Kamala said, cutting him off. "This is literally the last thing I need right now. I should be studying, not chasing after weird villains. Why can't you Avengers just leave me ALONE!"

She took off running down the street, seething with anger.

Kamala knew she had a bad temper. She shouldn't go around
yelling at Asgardian warriors—or anyone—like that. But it wasn't her
fault that she had powers. What if she didn't want to be a Super Hero?

BRRRRNG! Just then she heard alarms. A pet store was being
robbed! Kamala hung her head. Knowing she had to help, Kamala
quickly changed into her Ms. Marvel suit.

"Help! A Super Villain is robbing my store!" the owner shouted.

Ms. Marvel saw red. This evil thing was going to regret ever stepping foot in her city. She *stretched* one of her arms, grabbing the criminal. When Ms. Marvel got a good look at the villain, she gasped. Was that a . . . beak?

It screeched loudly. "Squawk! Squaaawk!"

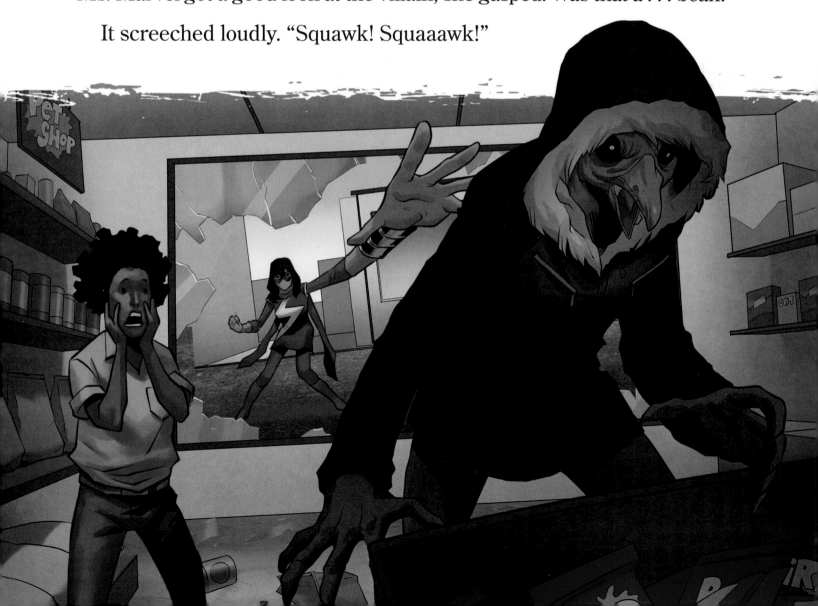

"Be *quiet*!" Ms. Marvel yelled, squeezing the creature a little too tightly. Suddenly, she heard the villain start to cry. Ms. Marvel released the creature, and it ran away.

Kamala took off her mask. She began to cry, too. What was she thinking? She could've really hurt someone. Silently Thor sat down beside her. "You know, you and I have a lot in common."

"I doubt it," Kamala replied.

"It's true," Thor said. "I used to have quite the temper, too."

Kamala wiped away a tear. "Really? Because from where I'm sitting, you seem pretty perfect. You're an Avenger."

"Even Avengers aren't perfect," Thor said, picking up Kamala's mask. "You let your temper get the best of you today. But it doesn't define who you are. Now come on, Ms. Marvel. I need your help. The Inventor is plotting world domination as we speak."

With that, Kamala gently picked herself up and grabbed Thor's hand. Then the heroes flew off, ready to fight.

CRASH! Ms. Marvel and Thor burst into the Inventor's lair. It was filled with bird-people! In a matter of seconds, they attacked in a flurry of feathers and a chorus of cheeps. The heroes kicked and punched—swung and spun—until Thor's lungs were heaving and Ms. Marvel's fists were aching.

"Oh, how wonderful! You came," said a sneering, shrill voice.

Ms. Marvel looked up. It was the Inventor! He was standing on top of some kind of giant robot.

"I bid you welcome," he said, ". . . to your doom."

"At least he's polite," Thor remarked brightly.

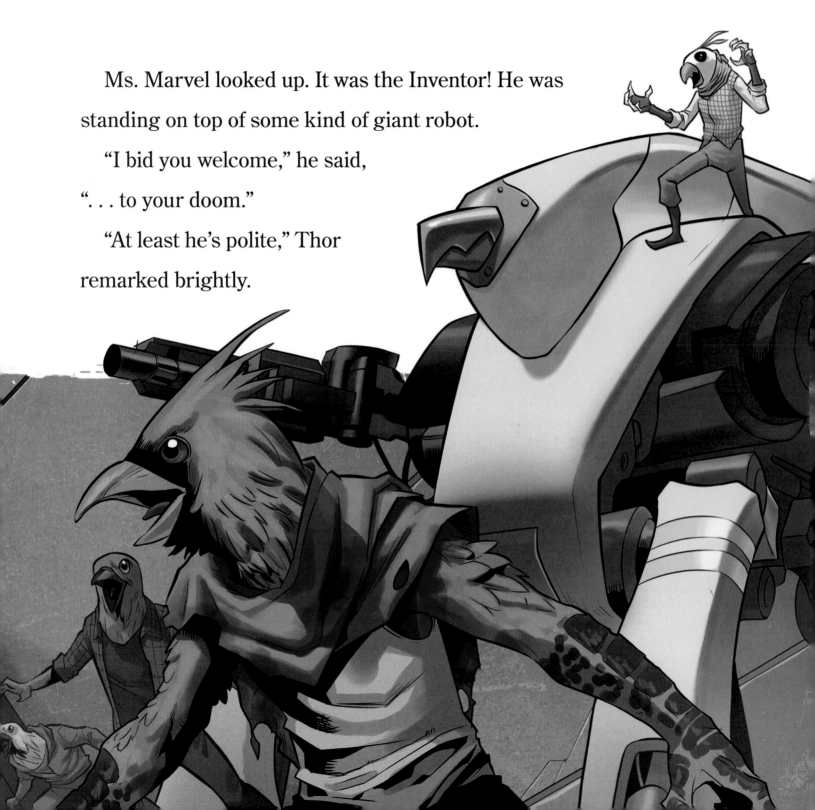

"Perhaps you're wondering what I am doing here," the Inventor said. "Well, make yourselves comfortable, and I shall tell—"

"You're stealing pet birds and putting their DNA into people you recruited for your villainous super-powered bird-army. Yeah, Thor told me on the way over here," Ms. Marvel said. Thor gave a hearty snort.

"Oh," the Inventor said, annoyed. "Yes, well. Got it in one."

"Let's move straight to the final showdown," Ms. Marvel said. She *embiggened* herself until she was nearly as high as the ceiling.

"You don't want to hear about my revolutionary new enzyme that divides nucleotides?" the Inventor asked, eyes wide with fear.

"No," Ms. Marvel replied, grabbing a huge machine. She smashed it into the Inventor's robot, completely destroying it! "Biology is sort of a sore subject for me right now."

They did it! Ms. Marvel and Thor had defeated the Inventor. But how were they going to fix all of these bird-people?

"Got it," Ms. Marvel said, pushing a big red REVERSE button on the MUTATOR 3000. Suddenly the room was full of normal people and exotic birds flying in confused circles.

"It has been an honor, Ms. Marvel," Thor said. "Call me if you ever again find yourself . . . stretched too thin."

Ms. Marvel smirked. "Your jokes are terrible. But I guess no one is perfect."

MARVEL AVENGERS

ISLAND OF THE CYBORGS

S *PLASH!* Captain America landed feetfirst in the churning ocean. He was several miles off the coast of an uninhabited island. He was there on a very important mission.

Two weeks ago, an ocean tanker carrying hundreds of robotic battle suits went missing. Then about a week later, monkeys from another small island began to vanish.

Cap was ready to investigate.

Battle suits. Islands. Monkeys. What's the connection? Captain America thought as he jogged to shore. Since joining the Avengers, solo missions were rare for Cap. He was nervous, but quickly shook it off as he found himself standing before a towering fortress. Cap listened to the palm trees swaying and the waves gently crashing.

PEW! PEW PEW! Suddenly the sky lit up with hundreds of bright green blasts—all intended for Captain America.

One of the powerful blasts threw Cap to the ground. He struggled getting up, straining to see through the dust and debris. Then he spotted a strange shape in the distance. "M.O.D.O.K.! I should have known."

M.O.D.O.K. was a genetically engineered super-intelligent being bent on destroying the world. But the Super Villain wasn't the only thing Cap recognized.

"You've got to be kidding me." He looked up to see the missing battle suits being piloted by the missing monkeys!

M.O.D.O.K. smiled. "Captain! So we meet again. Let's take a tour, shall we?"

Inside the fortress, Captain America was locked up as a prisoner. M.O.D.O.K. laughed outside his cell.

"Now you can watch as I take over the world with my new army!" M.O.D.O.K. said.

"Very original," Cap said. "And why the monkeys?"

"Primates are easy to control," M.O.D.O.K. replied.

Captain America scoffed. "Okay, so what're a few monkeys in metal tubes going to do?"

M.O.D.O.K. turned in his chair. "I wouldn't say a few."

M.O.D.O.K. flew out of the fortress to hover outside Cap's cell window. When the hero sat up to look, his eyes widened at the massive army of mechanical primates!

"Thousands of them," M.O.D.O.K. said. "State-of-the-art battle suits fitted with heat-seeking rocket launchers, dual-laser cannons, jet packs, and iron fists that could punch through a steel wall! All ready to do my bidding."

M.O.D.O.K.'s laugh echoed through the valley of cyborg monkeys!

Captain America sat back down in his cell, disheartened. But he couldn't give up. He needed to fight back! That gave him an idea.

"Hey, ugly!" Cap shouted at one of the cyborg monkeys walking by his cell. "I call this one Monkey See, Monkey Do!"

The hero began to slam his metal cuffs against the bars of the cell. The sound vibrated through the stone walls. The cyborg monkey started to twitch, and his mouth twisted into a terrifying smile. He was ready to attack!

The cyborg monkey reared its head—the loud noise was driving him crazy. He began to claw at the metal bars. Anything to make the sound stop. His battle suit bent the bars enough that he pulled himself inside the cell with Captain America. With a screech, the cyborg monkey lunged at the hero. Cap slid between the cyborg's legs, free from his prison cell!

In an instant, the rest of the cyborg monkeys attacked! Captain America didn't have time to doubt himself. He punched one cyborg and was surprised when the battle suit exploded! A frightened monkey quickly scurried out of the broken metal body. Suddenly, Cap remembered why he was here. *These poor animals . . . I'm their only way out of here,* he thought.

With renewed strength, Captain America set about destroying every cyborg in the lab. He had to free all the monkeys from M.O.D.O.K.'s mind control.

Taking off into the belly of the fortress, Captain America knew he had won the battle—but he had not yet won the war. From previous encounters with the villain, Cap knew M.O.D.O.K.'s chair was the key. If he could destroy the chair, he could destroy the mind control.

Suddenly, Cap heard voices coming from outside. He hid behind the wall and listened. It was M.O.D.O.K. talking to his cyborg minions!

"Tonight, I will begin a brand-new experiment when I use that nosy Avenger to test my mind-control battle suits. If all goes according to plan, I'll have my very own mind-controlled Super Soldier to do my evil bidding. He will have no choice but to do as I command!"

"Doesn't really sound like me," Captain America said, making his presence known.

M.O.D.O.K. gasped. "Cyborgs, attack!"

Captain America battled the cyborg monkeys with every ounce of his enhanced strength. Broken metal and confused monkeys were everywhere. The tide was turning against M.O.D.O.K. Realizing he was going to lose, the villain tried to retreat.

"Not so fast!" Captain America shouted.

The hero threw his Vibranium shield at M.O.D.O.K., sending the villain crashing into the ocean below. The still-suited cyborg monkeys suddenly woke up, freed from M.O.D.O.K.'s mind control. Cap looked over the wall for any signs of M.O.D.O.K., but he had vanished beneath the dark and powerful waves.

With M.O.D.O.K. gone, Captain America worked to release the remaining monkeys from their battle suits. Luckily, none of them were harmed. One by one they scurried off, happy to be free.

As Cap watched the sunrise, he was overcome with a feeling of accomplishment. He did it! Then he smiled as, moments later, he spotted the Quinjet headed his way.

"That's my ride," Cap said to no one in particular. "I can't wait to tell the Avengers about this one."